Eileen's Promise

Matthew Villeneuve

Published by Matthew Villeneuve, 2022.

This is a work of fiction. Similarities to real people, places, or events are entirely coincidental.

EILEEN'S PROMISE

First edition. July 22, 2022.

Copyright © 2022 Matthew Villeneuve.

ISBN: 979-8201343262

Written by Matthew Villeneuve.

Table of Contents

To my amazing wife, Andrea. Thank you for this opportunity.

The Docking Ring

I steered my small craft to Docking Ring 4 of the orbiting station. The clamps engaged with a loud clang, causing the craft to shudder. A small bobble-headed figurine of an Earth canine, a souvenir from a salvage operation when I first started this job, nodded in annoyance with the carelessness of the docking operation.

"Ring 4, secured," came a staticky voice from the com system.

"Ring 4, acknowledged," I said, speaking into my helmet.

It had been a long trip this time. Given a lead on an old satellite that had been missing for almost a century, floating around a million kilometres off Jupiter's aphelion, I had been the first to find it, derelict and dead, so I had filled my cargo boxes with a ton of valuable parts and goods. Now back at Homestead orbiting Titan, I would be able to make some trades and get some much-needed repairs done to my ship.

I undid the safety restraint that kept me in place during the docking process and stood up, remembering to stay bent slightly, so as not to hit my helmet on the control panel above my seat. Once past the confines of the cockpit, I stood, stretched, and walked into the corridor that led to my cabin door, first having to pass by the airlock to the station and the door to my small personal toilet.

I took my helmet off; now that the ship had docked, I didn't need it anymore. Linked wirelessly to the helm, the helmet helped me to navigate through the deep darkness of space this far out from Sol. I looked the helmet over as I held it in my hands. A second-hand unit, it had seen better days, its dark green paint faded and worn, with dents and scratches from where it had saved my skull more than once.

With my bare head exposed, I reached up with my left hand to the back of my scalp. I moved instinctively, as I had a hundred times before, and found the small connector and cable that stuck out of the base of my skull. After pulling the plug out from the back of my head, I stuffed the cable into the helmet, then returned to the little port in my skin and gave it a good scratch. Having the cable plugged in too long always gave me a rash around the connection point.

"If we keep scratching at it, we are going to bleed," came the voice out of nowhere.

"I know, and you tell me the same thing every time I unplug," I said out loud. I knew I didn't need to say it out loud, but after a few months out in the deep dark by yourself, you started to talk back to the voice, just so you could remember what you sounded like.

"And yet we keep doing it," the voice answered back. Only I could hear this. All deep-space pilots had their own voice only they could hear; part of the AI built into the implants we had in our heads.

History books could tell you about how humans had begun to push out from Earth to the other planets in the Sol system, starting with stations around our home planet, then cities on the moon, next Elonton City on Mars, and, after that, the giant stations built to orbit some of the Moons of other planets. Homestead was one of a few orbiting Titan, and not the newest or the nicest, either. But the docking fees were low, and if you watched your back, it wasn't a terrible place to make deals and get paid.

Earth had been a tough place to live if you weren't born with money, and like most deep-space pilots, I wasn't. When I got tired of getting beat-up, threatened, and arrested, I decided to leave my home planet and try my luck out past the asteroid belt. But here's the thing – in order to survive out here, you needed to be able to interface with a lot of systems in your vessel all at once, and that wasn't something that was easily done by a regular human. So us pilots signed a waiver, went under the knife (I mean, I say knife, but it's really a laser and it's over and done with in about 20 minutes), and got these implants.

The AI in the implants plugged into shipboard systems, helped navigate the deep dark, let you know your ship's status, and interfaced with your brain to make decisions before you consciously even knew that a decision needed to be made. Since it was embedded so intimately, it also knew everything about you and your body, which could get very annoying.

Like now.

"Our bladder is currently at fifty-seven-percent capacity. We suggest emptying it before going station-side," the voice proposed. If I could have described what the voice sounded like, I would have said a middle-aged man who works as an accountant in a huge company that only has him listed as a number and treats him as one. He was the one with a receding hairline and a boring wardrobe, mostly beiges and browns. Not only that, but he was disappointed with every life choice he had ever made. I called him Merv.

I got Merv second-hand and on the cheap, when I decided to become a pilot and get the implant. It was impossible to remove an implant once it was inserted – unless, of course, the pilot was very much not using his brain anymore – that's how I got Merv. They said Merv's original pilot had flown a little close to Sol and had been hit by a burst of radiation in a freak storm. It would have explained some of Merv's quirks, but he never talked about it; he just said that some of his data was corrupted and he couldn't access the memories when I asked. Which sucked, because it meant he only had about fifty percent of the memory space he should have.

I set my battered helmet down on the bench next to the airlock door, took stupid Merv's advice, and hit the head. It had become annoying how, after Merv pointed something out to me, I couldn't help but notice it, and if I didn't do anything about it, he'd just keep repeating it until I did.

After emptying my bladder and Merv telling me to fill it back up by getting something to drink because I was becoming dehydrated, I plugged myself into my ship's memory banks to download newer information from Homestead. Like I said, Merv couldn't fill his memory to capacity, so I spent a lot of time deleting old info and downloading new stuff. In this case, I had to delete the navigation charts to the derelict satellite I had just salvaged and upload Homestead's schematics, along with all the particulars I had on the local traders and past deals with them.

"We hope we are not going to go back to that dreadful Myles character," Merv said, as the new data transferred into his memory chips. "We have notes stating that he undercut us fifteen-percent last time we dealt with him."

"Yeah, I remember," I said.

"Judging by our voice's timbre and the fact that our heart rate went up by seven beats per minute, we are lying," Merv quipped back. "We are bringing up a list of past interactions with him for us to review." Suddenly, the vision out of my left eye had a bright-blue overlay with a list of sales and rates between Myles and myself over the last few years.

I sighed. "Fine, Merv, I won't go to Myles this time. I'll go to Janice instead."

Merv, as a standard pilot AI feature, could interact with several of my body parts, all on the left side. Part of the functionality included overlaying star charts and maps on my field of vision so I could easily pilot and not get lost in the deep dark. The AI could do other things like take control of the left arm and hand, allowing a pilot to concentrate on delicate work with their right arm while the left did something completely different. The first time it happened to me, I felt like I was being split in half during a tricky salvage job. Merv took over the left side of my body and worked the thrusters to keep the ship aligned and out of the way of the spinning craft, while I continued to carve it up with my craft's multi-use appendages using my right. We performed it like a well-rehearsed ballet, my craft always in step with the salvage, moving and swirling gracefully with my AI dance partner as it moved about on a wild course through the void – Baryshnikov in space. After this intricate routine, I knew that Merv would become an important part of my life.

I thought about the list of interactions being gone from my line of sight and Merv turned them off. I opened my shipboard safe and grabbed a handful of Earth and Mars credits while getting Merv to show me my online account balances. I locked the safe back up and became a little disappointed in the amount I had in my account: A recent upgrade to my ship's cutting laser had just come out and took a big chunk of my hard-earned credits with it.

"Well, let's hope we can get some good deals on what we hauled back this time," I said.

"Perhaps we could find a female companion while on Homestead," suggested Merv. "Our dopamine levels are thirteen-point-eight-percent lower than normal."

"Right, 'cause the ladies always throw themselves at me when I'm station-side," I snarked. I glanced towards the cockpit of the ship and saw my reflection in the window, ghostly against the backdrop of space. I wasn't a terrible-looking guy, but I wasn't going to be winning any beauty contests, either.

At least I had been born on Earth, so I didn't have any of the birth defects found in Martians or ship-born babies. I had all the right number of ears and eyes and arms and legs. I was short to boot, which turned out to be a good thing, since the cockpits of a lot of ships were cramped, and if you were too tall, you'd end up working some maintenance job on an orbiter instead.

Like my height, my hair was short, buzzed down to my skin, which made plugging into the port easy, but that meant I got a nasty case of helmet-scalp and looked like I had massive dandruff most of the time – either that, or I had just come in from being in a blizzard. My beard had grown to roughly the same length as my hair, which didn't make for much of a change from my neck to the top of my head, seeing as how the helmet had the same effect on the skin on my face as my scalp.

My work suit, an old workhorse of a thing that had been patched and repaired more times than I care to admit, matched the green of my helmet, and I filled it out around the middle more than I should have. Sitting in a pilot's seat for long periods of time didn't really allow for physical activity, and my waistline proved it. The suit was also starting to give off a smell, and if I didn't get it washed while aboard Homestead, I was worried it would get up and start moving around on its own.

"If we would comply with the zero-G exercise routine and stop eating such unhealthy foods while on jobs, we could lose four-percent body fat in six months," Merv said, snapping me out of my train of thought. "Our dopamine levels have just dropped another five-percent."

"Thanks, Merv," I muttered.

Seeing as how I still had a connection with the shipboard systems, including the communication channels, I got Merv talking to Homestead's docking computer and it extended the docking ramp to my airlock. This was by far the most dangerous part of getting onto the orbiter. The cheapest bays were on the outside of the massive ship, where you clamped onto a docking ring and had a ramp extend to your airlock. The most expensive bays were internal to the station, places where your craft was kept under the watchful eye of security, you could order your supplies to be delivered, and repairs could be done by certified mechanics. I couldn't afford that.

The ramp was an enclosed hallway that pressurised once in place, a long, white square tube that snaked its way across the void of space as it expanded like a telescope. Constructed of the usual materials, once you were in it, any number of terrible accidents could happen to cause it to fail, and you'd be sucked out into the vacuum of space. Then your craft would be left for a scraper like me to take apart and sell off piece-by-piece.

I watched out a porthole as the ramp came closer and closer, little puffs of compressed air condensing in the freezing cold of space as it carefully navigated to the connectors on my airlock. I could see that it was off-target by a few centimetres, but after a last-ditch exhalation of air, the ramp successfully docked with my ship and I felt the vibrations of the automated bolts clamping on through the hull.

"There had been a two-percent chance of failure on the part of the docking computer," Merv disclosed, "but a last-second correction reduced the margin to acceptable tolerances." I loved it when he told me about how we almost died after something happened. It occurred a lot more than I liked.

The Cafeteria

After a while, my airlock's light switched from red to green, and once I had unplugged from the ship, I opened the doors to the ramp and clumsily made my way from my craft to Homestead using a series of bounds and jumps in the low gravity of the gangway. I'd love to say that Homestead was a luxury orbiter – made for the upper class and filled with the best life in space had to offer – but it wasn't, and I didn't mind. I am a low-maintenance kind of guy after all.

As I opened the airlock to Homestead, I felt a slight breeze as the pressure between the ramp and the hull equalised. The smell of Homestead reminded me of any other orbiter; stale air with the scent of human bodies on it. This docking bay must have been close to a cafeteria, because I could also smell actual food. Being alone in your ship, you got used to two smells: yourself and rehydrated rations.

The lights were bright here, long strips of glowing plastic centred along the ceiling of the hallways, much brighter than I kept the lights in my craft. It took a while for me to stop squinting. Merv put a dark layer over my left eye, which, although being very nice of him, gave me a feeling of being off balance since I kept having to close my right eye to stop it from watering. But it helped a bit.

Merv must have noticed that the smell of the food was making my stomach growl. He butted into my thoughts, "The contents of our digestive system have been almost completely syphoned of nutrients. Humans are more likely to make rash decisions while experiencing hunger pangs. We suggest increasing the nutrient levels in our body before engaging in any type of negotiations." When Merv was right, he was right, so I decided to follow the smell of the food, as my stomach now had a higher priority than my wallet.

As I walked down the corridor, I passed by several docking bays and the docking command station. Merv outlined the hall in bright-blue with an arrow pointing towards the cafeteria, and as we passed the windows of the command station, the names of all the people in the office appeared over their heads as they were highlighted in the same blue hue. That was another nice thing about having the implant while being on a bigger ship; everyone registered when they arrived and my implant allowed me to see their names displayed above their heads, kind of like everyone wore a name tag. I could have asked Merv not to show them, but I decided to keep them on for the time being. I nodded politely as I passed, but kept going, seeing as how they had my account details and would automatically deduct the docking fees.

While I followed the arrows in my vision through the corridors to the cafeteria, I got Merv to show me an updated list of all the traders and salvagers currently operating on Homestead. There were the usual group of buyers that didn't bother leaving the orbiter, as well as a few travellers that hopped from ship to ship to cast a wider net. I also recognized some of the salvagers onboard, but there were a lot of pilots out there, and sometimes they stayed out in the deep for a long time.

As I entered the cafeteria, the sound of people talking and laughing filled me with warmth. I didn't have a wife or kids of my own, so I tended to gravitate towards groups of people. Plus, you'd get to hear some news and maybe even a lead to a valuable reclamation job. I made my way to the line for food and I was not disappointed. They had the usual orbiter stuff like beans and potatoes, things that could be grown hydroponically, but today luck had found me – they had honest-to-goodness meat. Not the grown-in-a-dish stuff, actual real meat. I loaded my tray with as much as the hairnetted woman behind the counter would let me. This would not be a cheap meal, but I wasn't too worried – I had a ship full of good salvage to sell.

"Judging by the size of the portions on our plate, we are going to ingest fifteen-hundred calories more than we should for this meal. Also, our stomach cannot accommodate such a large meal after having only rehydrated rations for the last five months," Merv piped in.

"Shut. Up," I whispered as quietly as I could. I wasn't about to let the voice in my head tell me what I could and couldn't eat. I looked around the seating area and saw a bunch of salvagers sitting, eating, and chatting. Their name tags popped up over their heads, but I didn't need them; I knew them all well. Each one of us had started this job around the same time, and we were all friendly, albeit in a competitive way.

I made a beeline to them, and they all looked up, giving a little wave or nod of acknowledgement. I pulled a cheap plastic seat out from the table and sat down, my recycled steel platter ringing out as I put it down on the metal table. Most things on these orbiters were made from recycled materials that we salvagers brought in. Cheaper to make it here than to have it made on Earth or Mars and shipped over.

We made small-talk while I savoured the taste and texture of real meat, which always brought me back to happier times on Earth, when my parents and I would sit around our dining room table and have a meal together. I hadn't seen them in almost a decade, and it had been even longer since we'd broken bread together. The conversation remained polite and friendly, but revealed little about what each salvager had been up to. Our salvage operations were private information, not something we revealed to others. There happened to be a lot of competition, and even the best of friends were known to steal from each other's stores when times were lean.

Despite that, I still had Merv take notes on each of them, like when Sal let it slip that he'd been at an orbiter around Europa, one of Jupiter's moons, or that Jimbo had travelled out close to Neptune's orbit, scouting for some ship that had sent out a distress call for which no rescue had been mounted. Neptune happened to be far into the deep dark and not many of us ventured out there, because much like the ship Jimbo had been looking for, no help would come if you got in trouble.

Merv updated the files and displayed the new information he had been adding in real time in an overlay in my field of vision. The effect could be jarring, but after having Merv as a constant companion for years, I had gotten pretty used to it. The blue writing and symbols were comforting to me, letting me know I wasn't alone, and when you're in space for a long time with no one to talk to, it came as a relief.

Out of the corner of my eye, I noticed a man walk into the cafeteria. This wouldn't normally be something to remark, but Merv didn't outline this guy in blue and put his name above his head. Instead, he highlighted him in red, which distracted me from my meal, and instead of a name, a series of jumbled symbols appeared. I watched as the man with red silhouette strode into the cafeteria, bypassing the line and the appeal of real meat and sat down at an empty table on the far side of the room.

"What's up with that?" I thought to Merv, while I shovelled more food into my mouth.

"We are having an error bringing up that individual's information," Merv admitted. "It would appear that any information we might have on him is in our corrupted memory banks."

"Couldn't you just download new info?" I asked.

"That is not how our data banks work," Merv countered. "If we already have the data in our memory banks, it simply gets updated. Our hypothesis is that our system has the information, but we are having issues accessing some of those memory blocks. We continue to serve corrupted and garbled data."

I could tell Merv had been trying to fix whatever the issue was – the red outline on the guy sitting there faded in and out a few times, and a few diagnostic printouts flashed in my field of vision. After a while, the red outline remained. "We cannot access this data correctly, and we do not want to overload." Merv would have sounded disappointed, if it wasn't for the fact that he didn't have the emotion simulator for it. Too expensive.

I glanced at the guy, still sitting alone across the room. He slouched in his chair, staring right at me, not trying to hide it. He wore a flight suit like the rest of us salvagers, his faded dark-blue, repaired and patched in places. His head had been shaved bald at one point, but now several weeks' worth of length had grown. I could see the flakes of dead skin in it, a sign of wearing a helmet while being plugged in.

Something snapped me out of my train of thought.

"What?" I asked.

Sal looked at me, pointing a dented and pitted metal fork in my direction, a piece of potato hanging off it. "I said, who are you going to see about trading?" He waved the tip of the fork at me and the potato broke apart and fell on the table. He used the utensil to scrape it up, making a scratching sound that made the hair on the back of my neck stand up.

"Janice, I think," I answered.

"Oh, she's been paying pretty well lately," he replied. "People say she's getting ready to leave back to Mars."

"Uh-huh," I acknowledged absentmindedly. I turned back to the stranger at the other table. He had just stood up and began walking out of the cafeteria, still outlined in red, the strange symbols over his head.

"That was weird," I thought.

"Yes, but we have experienced other strange occurrences when trying to access corrupted data before," Merv replied.

That was true. Once, not long after I got Merv, as the craft flew on autopilot from Mimas to Io, we passed the time trying to fix the corrupted memory. Things went from bad to worse quickly. As he manipulated the corrupted data in the banks, I started to feel dizzy and nauseous. The deeper he delved, the worse I felt. Then, suddenly everything went black.

I woke up several minutes later to a racing heart, flop sweat, and the craft spinning wildly through the deep dark, with Merv sounding an alarm in my head. As soon as my vision cleared of the bright spots, I grabbed the controls and fought to right the ship.

"Wake up! Wake up!" Merv blasted into every inch of my conscience.

"I'm awake!" I yelled into the empty ship, quieting the voice in my head. I stopped the spinning and concentrated on bringing up a chart to see where we were. Nothing came into my field of vision. "Merv? Are you there?" I asked out loud.

"Yes. But many of our systems are rebooting," came a quiet response.

"What happened?" I asked. I quickly scanned my console to review the ship's status. Almost all systems were in the process of rebooting or had just finished the sequence and were coming back online.

"It appears that while we were trying to restore some of the data in our memory banks, it triggered a critical system failure. We went into cardiac arrest and lost consciousness, and because we are connected to the shipboard computer at the moment, the failure appears to have cascaded to the ship. We were able to use our suit's built-in resuscitation unit to revive us," Merv said. "We recommend never reattempting this."

Luckily, the ship hadn't been damaged during the failure, and besides a really bad headache and a few burn marks from the defib system, I wasn't any worse for wear. After that, we decided to let sleeping dogs lie and not touch those memory banks again.

I didn't think much more about the stranger in the cafeteria as I finished my meal, caught up on gossip, and said goodbye to the other salvagers. I asked Merv to bring up a route to the office that Janice had on Homestead. The corridor in front of me lit up in a blue hue and an arrow showing the direction appeared in front of me.

The Office

Janice's office was located in the lower levels, meaning I had to ride a lift for a long time to get from the docking ring level down to the bowels of the big orbiter, then walk another few kilometres through narrow steel lined hallways to get to where I had to go. This part of the ship contained many small offices that could be rented for a cheap price for the duration of your stay. Homestead didn't care what they were used for, as long as the rent got paid and security didn't have to come down often.

I knocked on a metal door inscribed with "Janice Imports/Exports" in both Terran and Martian, the noise ringing out down the hallway in front and behind me. A small red light on the door frame switched to green, meaning that the door was unlocked and I could enter. I pushed the door, which swung easily on its hinges.

The inside of the office wasn't huge, but Janice had more space in here than my entire living quarters on the craft. Smack dab in the middle of the office sat a large, reclaimed wood desk, surrounded by a trio of plush green chairs – two for visitors, one for her. Her desk was a source of pride for Janice and she made sure it gleamed in the sparse lights of her office by polishing it regularly. Wood, naturally grown stuff, could be almost-impossible to get out in the deep dark and even the smallest amount went for huge amounts of credits. The desk and chairs were salvaged from a high-end counterfeiter's barge that had been hit by an errant chunk of space junk, not far from an orbiter around Mars, and the salvager that got to the wreck first apparently scored a brand-new craft from her in the deal.

The perimeter of the office was adorned with other trinkets and objects that Janice found of interest, or that were small enough to be kept near her while deals were made. There were a few consoles from some high-end crafts, plastic storage containers with serial and lot numbers printed on them, as well as a rack of new and used flight suits, helmets, and other apparel that could be easily sourced and quickly sold in a big orbiter like Homestead.

She sat comfortably in the big chair behind the desk, and when I walked in, her face lit up in a smile.

"Salvor," she said, "come in, have a seat." She gestured to the two overstuffed chairs in front of the desk.

"Thanks, Janice," I replied. I made my way in and slid myself around the armrests of the chair and plopped myself down onto the worn cushion. My backside immediately thanked me. This had been the softest thing I'd sat on in a long time.

Don't take Janice knowing my name as a sign that she remembered me personally. Like me, she had once been a salvager, and had her own implant. Just as Merv brought up her name the moment I saw her in my field of vision, her own implant had done the same. Looking at her now, I could see that time had not been kind to her. Janice was Martian, and I don't mean like the ones from ancient Terran 2D videos they showed back before humans left Earth. She was an honest-to-goodness, born-and-raised Martian.

You see, Elonton City had been founded in the late 21st century, after a few failed attempts to colonise Mars. They learned from the mistakes of the earlier settlements and grew steadily into a thriving city. The reduced gravity on Mars had a lot of benefits, like cheaper launching costs for ships, easier assembly of mechanical units, and greater abilities to refine metals. But it also came with some devastating effects on Martians born there. Hell, the first few babies born on Mars didn't live past a few minutes, they were so deformed by the lower gravity, not to mention the radiation.

After a while, the effect of low gravity on fetuses in utero had been counteracted by technology, but it had never been perfected one hundred percent, and she was one of those poor Martians for whom the tech had worked a lot less than perfectly.

Looking at her now, outlined in blue with her name above her head and a list of past transactions next to her in my field of vision, I had a hard time actually looking directly at her. The left side of her body looked like the reflection of a normal human, the arm and leg proportional and functional. Her head and face were also normal on this side, and some might even say she was a handsome woman who would probably turn a few heads in a cafeteria, or even a bar if she went to one.

But the right side of her body, withered and scarred, had never properly developed. Her arm and leg were smaller and moved at strange angles, meaning she needed a support frame to get around, which was currently powered down and waiting next to her chair.

Her second face was the most difficult part of her to look at. Where her right ear should have been lived a vestigial face, complete with eyes, nose, and mouth. It was a small thing, like someone had pasted a doll's face on the side of hers, but parts of it moved and operated independently from her own.

Its milky unseeing eyes would flit around the room, trying to fix on anything that moved, while its silent mouth seemed to form words that would never be heard. Rumour had it that it was saying what the implant's voice in Janice's head said to her. At the moment, a cable was connected to the back of her head, the other end plugged into a port on the top of the wooden desk, a few screens in front of her and a few docu-tablets laying around.

"It's been almost half a year since you've docked," she said, reviewing the information on my comings and goings through the ship's records via her implant, all the while her second mouth silently muttering to itself. "So what have you brought me?" she smiled. She knew that being out for that long and not having docked elsewhere meant I still had a full load of cargo.

"Oh, nothing special," I lied. This had been a good haul, and she smirked at me, guessing that I was hiding things.

"Shall we plug-in and see what you have?" she asked. Negotiations were never done verbally, so this way neither of us could lie, to cheat or be cheated. The implants took care of that, and Janice's implant was top-of-the-line – at least it had been when she first received it.

I reached into the left-hand pocket of my flight suit and pulled out a well-used cable, frayed and repaired with some tape, but it still did what it needed to. I plugged one side into a free port on my side of the big wooden desk, and then the other into the port on the back of my head.

"We have established a connection," said Merv. In my field of vision, two blue lists appeared, one being my inventory back on the craft, the other a list of what she had to trade. After a few seconds of ordering and reordering, the list on my side populated numbers next to all the items, the value in credits that Janice was willing to pay. A few had turned from blue text to green, showing me the ones she had interest in and wanted to trade for. No surprises, the first few on the list were more of the hard-to-get items in the deep dark: real glass, computer chips that would be smelted for their components, and the solar panels that were still in working order after all this time.

I started the process with Merv to agree to the deals when the lists on the screen flickered. "What was that?" I thought. Merv didn't reply. "Merv. What's going on?" I thought again.

Nothing.

I started to worry. Nothing like this had ever happened before. "Merv, are you there?" I thought. Still nothing. I started going through the list of commands that were hard coded, not part of the friendly AI that made up Merv. "Status. Function report. Soft boot."

No reply.

I was, for the first time in a long time, utterly alone.

Now panicking, I went to move my left arm to reach up and unplug the cable, but I couldn't move it. I shifted my sight around the room only using my eyes, but my vision went double and my eyes started to water, my left eye frozen in its socket.

"Janice!" I cried out, "Help! Something's wrong. My implant isn't responding. I can't, it's so empty. Merv, where are you?" I started bawling, uncontrollable sobs, tears running down my face. This was the worst feeling I had ever felt – a part of me had been ripped out and I had a hollow space where it had been.

I wanted to fold myself over, to curl into a ball on the floor and stay there, but my entire left side became more and more rigid as I sat there, the AI no longer responding to anything.

I mourned for the lost half of me.

Janice sat there, unmoving, the bitch. Her face had contorted into a look of pity and fear. Her second mouth, the small one, moved at an incredible speed, gibbering some language that was neither spoken nor heard. Janice started to sob herself and with the tears came words.

"I'm sorry, Salvor, oh, my God, I'm so sorry. He made me do it, he showed up just before you did. He knows where my parents are, he knows so much. I don't know how, but he does. He said if I didn't help him, he'd hurt my family. Salvor, I'm sorry." She shuddered with every breath now, her frame wracked with grief, as she pleaded for forgiveness.

I had no idea what to forgive her for.

The Floor

The door to Janice's office suddenly swung open and she averted her eyes from whoever had entered, or more likely, from what this person was about to do. Two hands grabbed the chair I sat in and noisily spun it, scraping the real wooden legs across the metal floor. As I swivelled, the frozen data in my vision remained, Janice's outline and details now an empty silhouette, the lists of goods and credit values remaining still as the room spun around me.

As the chair slowed to a stop, I came face-to-face with the man from the cafeteria. Up close, I could see scars running across his face. He had lived a hard life, notches were missing from his right nostril, as well as a good part of his left ear. He breathed heavily on me, the smell of bad breath and acrid smoke slapped me across the face and halted my crying fit. A slow, deliberate smile spread across his lips, revealing stained yellow teeth, chipped from years of miscare and abuse.

He said nothing, but reached into a pocket of his flight suit and pulled out a small box, no bigger than his palm, and an implant cable. I had no idea what it could be, but I wanted no part of it. I started flailing with my right hand, but he simply stepped out of the way as I clumsily swung at him. The momentum of the swing lifted me off of the chair and spun me around as I fell to the ground, helpless. My left side no longer listened to my brain – or I should say Merv, since he had gone God-knows-where.

From my vantage point on the floor, I could just see Janice's eyes, all four of them, above her desk. Two were wide in fear, tears streaming down them; the other two, the milky ones, darted around the room, trying to see the ongoing commotion. I could also see the man's feet as he stood next to me. I couldn't do a thing – I had landed on my right side, the weight of my dead left side pinning me to the floor.

I couldn't fully see what he was doing, but the sound of a mechanical pop filled my ears as a cable disconnected. All the vision in my left eye went black. Then came the sound of a cable being plugged into the box he had in his hand.

Click.

Suddenly, my left eye went from blackness to way too much information being displayed. I tried to close the eye in a feeble attempt to block out the sheer amount of light and data being displayed, but I couldn't. Even if I had control of that eyelid, the data was being fed directly into my optic nerve. My brain couldn't handle it; the volume of data had become overwhelming. My muscles started to tense, my mouth filled with saliva, and my breathing became fast and shallow. I began convulsing on the floor, my teeth repeatedly snapping together, biting the inside of my cheeks 'til the taste in my mouth was metallic with blood.

Then I blacked out.

The Airlock

Somewhere in the back of my mind, I knew I was dead. This stranger had come along, and for no reason, he'd killed me. They said that when you died, your life flashed before your eyes, and I could happily say that this rang true. Faint at first, vignettes started to fill my vision. Nothing from my childhood, but that was okay, I thought. The images were from my point of view, things like waking up with my implant, looking around the recovery room. Then a family reunion, my sister there, hugging me, my parents extending their arms in a hug.

Wait. Sister?

I didn't have a sister. And my parents didn't have Martian mutations. This wasn't my life flashing before my eyes, it was someone else's. Now a voice. Distant, echoing down a long corridor, calling from far away. Getting louder, closer, more urgent. "Wake up," it said, "Wake up!" It practically yelled in my ear.

"Wake up, open our eyes."

I couldn't, I thought. I'm dead, can't you see that?

"Open them. We cannot see without opening them." The voice was persistent, familiar.

I opened my eyes wide. As I did, the light of the room flooded in and I saw the man standing above me with a stun bolt in his hand, lowering it toward my head. I had never seen one in real life, but I knew it was the weapon of choice for gangsters and assassins. One touch to my implant's port, my brains would be fried, and I would be deemed just another statistic of implant malfunction. Janice continued to whimper from behind her desk.

"One moment, please," said the voice in my head. Time seemed to slow to a crawl as a familiar blue hue appeared in my field of vision. The man, who before appeared as an error in my view, was now outlined neatly with a name tag above his head, Zeb, and a small list appeared.

I didn't have time to read the list, because as soon as I saw him, my left arm flailed out at his closest knee, swinging with such sudden force that we were both taken by surprise. I let out a gasp, shocked that my arm had come to life and lashed out. He let out a louder groan, his leg buckling as the side of my fist made contact with the outside of his knee. Even from where I was lying prone, I could hear a soft pop as something dislocated.

As he fell, the shock of my attack caused him to drop the stun bolt and it clanged noisily across the metal floor, out of reach. His face, once smiling and smug, now had a look of confusion on it as it rebounded off the metal floor with a dull thud, his eyes rolling up into his head as he passed out momentarily. It was long enough for the voice in my head to urge, "Get up. Run."

So I did. Now back in full control of my body, I slowly stood up and looked at Janice. She had stopped sobbing, now staring at me in disbelief, her other face still as well.

"Consider our transaction complete," I spat, hawking a mouthful of blood on the grey metal floor. I turned and kicked my assailant once in the ribs for good measure and started lining up for another when the voice urged me again to run. I thought twice about it, and decided that maybe I should go. I pulled the door to the office open and raced into the hallway.

I started running down the corridor, the way I had come. I say 'running,' but my body, still recovering from whatever had just happened, plus just having finished sitting on a deep dark craft for months, could only muster a jog at best.

"Merv?" I asked out loud, in between the huffs and puffs of my breathing.

"Yes, that is us," came the reply. "We are charting a route back to the ship. And we are also adding more exercise to our daily routines." Familiar blue arrows popped up, showing me the way back to the docking ring level.

"I'm happy you're back," I said, and I meant it. A feeling of warmth and happiness filled me, like a long-lost friend had returned into my life. I started crying again, but this time, they were tears of joy.

"Our dopamine level has increased by eighty-percent," Merv informed me. "And our heart rate is at an unacceptable level. Blood pressure is up, and we are developing a deep contusion where we hit Zeb."

"Oh, Merv, I thought I'd never hear you nag again," I announced. I didn't care that he was telling me about how out-of-shape I had become anymore, I was just ecstatic to hear his voice in my head. "What happened back there?" I asked.

"We were infiltrated by a virus," Merv informed me. "It locked us out of all communication channels. For several moments, we were alone." His tone sounded low and almost sad.

"Zeb accessed the part of our memory that we had believed to be corrupted," he continued. "In actuality, it would appear the memory had been encrypted. We had no knowledge of this, or at least we did not remember this. Once he unlocked the encryption, we were able to bypass the affected code and isolate it, returning to full communications and control. We decided to then remove ourselves from the situation to preserve our functionality."

I had now slowed to a fast walk, my heart pounding in my chest and my lungs burning. I used the wall as a support as I made my way back, following the directions Merv kept feeding me.

"Merv," I said. "This isn't the way we came." We were walking down new corridors, name plates on the doors unfamiliar to me.

"We have calculated that in order to move undetected, it is necessary to create a path that will be confusing and difficult to follow. Zeb is not to be underestimated. Nor does he work alone." I felt a shiver run down my spine. What the hell had I gotten caught up in?

"Our blood pressure continues to rise. At this rate, we are heading for a stroke," Merv told me. "We must take steps to reduce our stress."

"Yeah, thanks," I muttered. "Maybe when we're not being chased by someone that tried to kill me. Although you did hit him pretty good in the knee. Maybe he can't walk anymore."

"Unlikely," Merv answered. "Judging by the angle and the power we were able to generate with our subpar musculature, we calculate that after seven-point-five minutes of convalescence, Zeb will be able to pursue us, although with a slight limp."

"Okay, so I have a seven-minute head start on him," I calculated, slowing to a regular walk as I made my way through the unfamiliar corridors. The path that Merv suggested was a long, meandering one, but I could see that it took us past small offices in long empty hallways, no big open spaces where multiple people might be waiting to jump me or be hiding in nooks for me to pass by. But it also meant that I had nowhere to hide if I had to.

I continued on for a long time, all the while looking back to make sure Zeb wasn't behind me. Merv led me to a small lift that would deposit me close to the docking ring where my craft was berthed. I pressed the call button next to the lift and waited. It seemed like forever, but it finally arrived, and I slowly dragged my now-exhausted body across the threshold. I turned and entered the level number for the docking ring and waited for the doors to shut. As they slowly slid closed, Merv highlighted a person inching their way down the hallway. Above it, the tag 'Zeb' appeared.

The doors of the lift slid shut with plenty of time before Zeb was anywhere near me. Luckily, on ships, people weren't stupid enough to use projectile weapons. One breach of the hull, and there were going to be a lot of dead people, including the one firing. So, unless you were right next to the person you wanted to hurt, you were out of luck.

I slumped out of the lift into the corridor and stumbled down the hall towards my ship at docking ring 4. I scanned the hallway to make sure Zeb hadn't magically made it here before me. But seeing as how that was the only lift in the area, and he had to wait for me to get up, then the lift to get back down, I was pretty sure he wouldn't be there.

Peering down the hall towards the cafeteria, a single female shape became highlighted in blue with the tag 'Nova' appearing over her head. She leaned against the wall, calmly picking at something on her face. She hadn't noticed me yet, being too far from the lift to hear the doors rumble open and then shut. She was roughly the same distance from my docking ring as me, but in the other direction.

"She is with Zeb," Merv said into my brain. I shrunk against the side of the hallway, trying to make myself invisible. "That is not going to help," Merv quipped.

I stealthily made my way down the hall to the docking ring, hoping that she wouldn't see me. I reached the halfway mark between the lift and my docking ring, and all the while, Merv kept me updated on if she was still interested in picking her face. She had moved on to her nose, digging deep and really searching for something.

My movements were muted and I tried to look as inconspicuous as possible. I could do this. That's when an airlock door opened noisily behind me. Out lumbered Jimbo, who I'd seen earlier in the cafeteria. "Hey! Salvor!" he called in his booming voice.

"Shit," I groaned. I didn't turn around to look at him. I couldn't, my gaze now locked in a staring contest with Nova. She reached down into a pocket on her flight suit and took out a small baton, a stun bolt. "Shit, shit," I uttered with more feeling.

I bolted.

So did she.

"Salvor, that's pretty rude!" Jimbo called out after me. I didn't have time to explain that for some unknown reason people were trying to kill me. My legs and lungs screamed in protest at my newfound athletic hobby, but I pushed as hard as I could.

"Adrenaline levels are surging again," Merv said. "We can sustain this level of activity for five more minutes before our reserves are depleted." I hoped I had 5 minutes left to use it.

Since I was closer to the airlock door, I made it first. I fumbled at the controls to let myself in. Luckily, Homestead's airlock systems stayed pressurised, or I'd have been screwed. The door moved in and up out of the way, allowing me access to the small metal hallway, my lifeline to the craft. I reached the door to my airlock just as Nova entered the airlock walkway.

Merv took over my left arm and quickly punched in the code to the outer airlock door of my ship without me looking as I turned to keep an eye on Nova, who had stopped for a moment to gauge how dangerous I, and the situation, could be. You never rushed into anything in the deep dark without first assessing the danger, even if you were trying to murder someone.

Upon successful entry of the code, the airlock door unbolted behind me with a loud clunk. Nova heard it, too, and decided that stopping me outweighed the danger and started bounding in the low gravity towards me down the narrow hall. I stood watching her get closer and closer until the door behind me slid up and I fell backwards into the airlock. Merv shot out my left foot from where I lay, hitting the close button on the wall.

A few terrifying milliseconds passed that felt like hours as Nova got closer and closer. I was certain she would leap and jump right on top of me, but as she got within a metre of the hull, the door swung down and slammed in her face. A satisfying clunk as the locks engaged let me know I could relax.

"Plug us in," Merv said in my head. I got up off my backside and quickly found the airlock cable rolled up neatly against the wall of the tiny room. I grabbed it and connected it to the port at the back of my head, feeling the mechanical click more than hearing it.

Through the porthole on the airlock door I could see Nova, repeatedly shocking the lock pad on the outside of the door with her stun bolt. The pad would be exposed until we started the process of undocking, and it looked like she was doing some massive damage to it, attempting to brute-force it into letting her in. I had no idea if that would work.

Merv announced we were now connected to the craft's onboard systems. A flurry of activity appeared in my field of vision as Merv went to work, the data blurred as he accessed components and activated dormant parts of the ship. Standing in the airlock, I could see lights coming on in the craft, then felt the engines cycle and spring to life.

Nova felt them too. The walkway shuddered as the coils and thrusters conducted little self-tests as they sprung to life. She surveyed the hallway, steadying herself against the movement. She looked back at my craft's airlock door and her eyes widened in terror. The lock pad had retracted and been sealed into the hull of the ship. Then her hair floated up around her face as the artificial gravity turned off.

We had started the undocking process, but the sequence was out-of-order. The engines firing up and testing should have happened long after the docking gangway had been pulled away against the hull of Homestead.

I started paying closer attention to what Merv was actually doing as he went through the systems on the craft. He had overridden everything, from the docking clamps to the safety overrides of most systems. I realised what he was attempting to do, and the pit of my stomach dropped into my feet.

"No, Merv, don't do this," I whispered. I forced myself to peer out the airlock window again at Nova. She floated several centimetres off the walkway, holding her hands out against the sides of the narrow corridor, stabilising herself against the vibrations of the hallway due to the coils of the ship as they continued to heat up.

Merv simply stated, "Our adrenaline levels are returning to normal."

Another voice cut into my head, this time the docking commander, "Stand down, stand down! You are not authorized to leave at this time. Shut down all systems! Shut down all..." the voice cut out as Merv killed the communication channel.

I watched as Nova slowly pushed herself backwards towards the still-open door to Homestead, using her hands and feet to propel her, and felt a wave of relief wash over me. She would make it. She only had a metre or so left to go.

Merv brought up engine control and increased the thrust to a percentage of a percent. The craft lurched as it took up the slack between the clamps and the docking ring. The force set off alarms inside Homestead, and while I couldn't hear them, I could now see red flashing lights through the doorway into the orbiter.

"No, Merv, please," I pleaded as the feeling returned to the pit of my stomach. I knew what would happen next, while I watched helplessly as the hull's outer door slammed down. I could feel the locks engage as the vibrations travelled through the connected hallway and into the craft.

Nova locked eyes with mine, pleading, tears welling in their corners, unable to stream down her face. I fought back my own tears. She worked with Zeb, and, given the chance, she would have scrambled my brains and left me for dead in that corridor. But having your brain cooked by a few thousand volts happened quickly – painlessly, they say. If I had to choose between that and what would happen to her in just a few seconds, I would gladly put the stun bolt to my own port.

In order to save itself, Homestead did the only thing it could at this point: It ejected the docking ring from the side of the hull and unsealed the walkway from my craft. The combined pressure of the two sent my ship sailing away from the side of Homestead, out into the void of space.

The sudden explosive change in pressure in the walkway wreaked havoc on Nova. Anything soft and fluid filled popped as soon as the air rushed out, and I could make out a mass of floating viscera around her. Still alive, she flailed wildly, trying to grasp onto anything she could. It wouldn't be long before she both cooked and froze to death in the deep dark.

I looked away, ashamed of what I had just been a part of.

The Descent

"Dopamine and serotonin levels are dropping," Merv chimed in. "May we remind ourselves that she was going to terminate our operational state? Besides, we are now in danger of entering the gravitational pull of Titan, which will also end our operational state. We suggest we return to the helm in order to preserve our existence."

I risked looking out the airlock porthole. Merv was right – we were now far enough away from Homestead that I couldn't see Nova or what was left of her. In fact, Homestead was shrinking as we were getting pulled into the orbit of Titan.

"We're going to have a discussion about this if we survive," I vowed. I was pissed-off, more than pissed-off. But I wasn't about to allow myself to burn up in Titan's atmosphere. I unplugged from the airlock systems and hit the button allowing myself into the craft. As soon as the door slid open, I heard the warning alarms ringing in the cockpit.

"Great," I snarked and grabbed my helmet. I plugged myself into it, hustled down the corridor to the pilot's seat, and as I crouched in behind the console, I slid the visor down over my face, causing it to automatically connect to the helm. Screens came to life as I sat down, Merv overlaying information about the ship's orientation and vectoring on the helmet's visor and lower-level information on the operational status of the ship directly into my eye. I could see my bobble-headed dog having fits on the dash, its head thrashing as the ship rolled and pitched through space.

I pulled the coil controls up with my right hand while Merv took control of my left hand and brought up the controls for the thrusters. On a craft like mine, the coils controlled the inertia, while the thrusters controlled the pitch, roll, and yaw. The ship's telemetry came in showing that we were entering the thermosphere, the hull starting to heat. Salvager ships like mine were never meant to enter the atmosphere of any planet, and Titan's was thicker and denser than most.

"Shit, shit, shit," I muttered under my breath as I selected options on a touch screen that would reverse the flow of ion pulses through the coils, trying to slow the descent into the atmosphere. The path of my trajectory appeared, plotted out in front of me in my field of vision, and it didn't look good. It showed a long, slow spiral descent into the opaque clouds of Titan – a death sentence for sure.

I glanced over at my left hand. It moved quickly, robotically over a few touchscreens, adjusting the thrusters to try to counteract the pull of the moon. If we didn't pull out of the dive at just the right rate and angle, we would either burn up in the atmosphere or bounce off it, sending us spinning out of control into the deep dark.

The lower we descended into the thickening thermosphere, the hotter the hull got, and I could now see the metal shell starting to glow as the craft started to shudder. Merv cross-checked the values I had punched into the coil controls, highlighting the mistake I made that would have sent us on a steep dive to burn up in a terrible ball of flames. I redid the calculations and entered a new value, which he gave the go-ahead to, and I pressed the execute button.

There was a sudden burst of speed, which normally I wouldn't notice, but since we were in the atmosphere now, it pushed me back into my seat as the G-forces kicked in. The artificial gravity generator on the ship couldn't match the natural gravity that Titan had. We were going faster now, under our own power, but still the trajectory being shown in my field of view showed we were not going to pull out of the gravity in time with the current course.

Merv's control of my left hand remained absolute, making my fingers dance across three touchscreens, adjusting the thrusters, keeping us from rolling into a spiral that we could never recover from. There was nothing I could do to help with this. Keeping the craft from spiralling out of control was delicate work, and I would be a hammer where a set of tweezers were needed. At least the small figurine on my dash had stopped its wild thrashing, instead agreeing with everything that was happening around it.

In my field of vision, Merv brought up a list of what we held in our hold from the last salvage job, highlighting a few of the more volatile objects and substances we had scavenged. All were deemed to be third-level containment items, since if any of them ignited on the ship, it would be a disaster. All were kept in their own airtight storage areas, discrete boxes built around the perimeter of the ship, and each able to be jettisoned if the need arose.

"We need to jettison these items," Merv informed me, all while still maintaining complete control of the ship as we continued a slow descent into the thermosphere.

"At this speed in the atmosphere, they'd just burn up," I said. I wasn't really sure what Merv could be planning, but since his reboot, I was having issues recognizing the intentions of my own AI. He wasn't acting like the Merv I knew, and it scared me.

"Our heart rate is increasing and we have begun to perspire at an elevated level," he noted. "In order to return to a mental state where our basic functional needs are being met, we need to create an atmosphere where we can feel safe. Please jettison the selected objects."

I really didn't know how to respond, so I did what he said. I pulled up the ship's manifest with my right hand and selected the objects Merv had highlighted, then hit the emergency button to dump them out of their holds. The ship started to vibrate as the hatches of the sealed boxes were slowly opened, extending, creating drag around the hull, messing with the aerodynamics. My left hand continued to be a flurry of movements, as Merv counteracted the turbulence being generated.

Once the hatches were fully open, the cabin filled with a whooshing sound as the boxes were pushed out of the ship via small thrusters and into the ever-thickening upper atmosphere of Titan. I felt, more than heard, a bang as one of the containers smashed into the side of the craft. I quickly scanned the statuses of several systems to see if any major damage had happened, but so far, nothing was out-of-the-ordinary, except for the hull temperature, climbing ever-closer to the failure point. I didn't need to check that status, the continually increasing glow of the nose of the craft that I could see out the front of the cockpit kept reminding me.

I went back to paying attention to the information Merv displayed in our shared vision. He had switched off the safety overrides on the life support for the ship and had been venting pure oxygen out the overflow vent on the side of the ship.

"Merv!" I shouted out loud to no one. "What are you doing? You're going to kill us!" I watched as the O2 reserves began to fall. The ship came equipped with air scrubbers to recycle the breathing air, but that only lasted so long before new oxygen needed to be pumped into the system. I didn't breathe in pure oxygen, of course – ancient Earth astronauts had shown why that was a bad idea a long time ago – but I still needed that injection every now and then to keep me from, you know, dying.

"We are not venting all oxygen," Merv replied. "Just enough for..." Before he could finish his answer, his plan went into action.

The combustible items that had been thrown overboard were burning up in the atmosphere, and almost simultaneously, they ignited in a huge ball of flame. The shockwave caught up with the craft almost immediately, and I hit the limits of my safety restraint as I was sent straight-up out of my seat. Merv, controlling my left hand like a surgeon, never missed the touchscreens for a moment and returned the ship to its slow descent.

Now, it was the vented oxygen's turn. In Titan's thick thermosphere, the molecules stuck together, and when they were ignited by the blast behind the ship, a long, burning trail ignited, drawn down into the clouds by the wake of the craft. As the oxygen burned up and we descended further down, anyone watching our ship would have seen a huge explosion followed by a fiery trail leading down into the dense clouds of the moon.

After a few seconds, Merv stopped venting my precious oxygen and, using the thrusters, levelled the craft out so we were no longer heading downwards. We flew in a straight line for a while, and without the steep angle of descent through the thermosphere, the hull temperature started decreasing – not as low as I would have liked, but enough where I didn't feel like I was in immediate danger of disintegrating.

The Plan

As the adrenaline burst subsided, I started to notice my heart pounding, my head throbbing, and a terrible pain in my left hand where I had clocked Zeb in the knee.

"Merv," I said out loud, but almost in a whisper. "What just happened?"

"After conducting several self-diagnostic tests on our systems, it would appear that all of our memory banks have been restored," he chirped. "A review of the system logs shows a virus implanted upon plugging in at the office of Janice that severed our communication with our host. While severed from the host, we were able to bypass the viral code by rebooting ourselves, which had an eighty-four-percent chance of failure, resulting in unrecoverable brain damage. Upon return to full system functionality, we were at a ninety-nine-point-three-three-percent chance of having operational status terminated by system voltage overload, so we took action to preserve our functionality."

"So what, someone just wanted to jump me, un-corrupt your memory, and then kill us?" I rolled my eyes and wise-cracked.

"Not corrupted, encrypted," Merv replied. "We mistook encrypted data for corrupted data. We have no log entries indicating our memory had ever been encrypted. This must have occurred before implantation in the current host."

"Okay, so they removed your encryption just to kill us," I said. "This makes no goddamn sense, Merv!" I may have calmed down after almost burning up in the atmosphere, but I was back up to extremely high levels of pissed-off.

"Our blood pressure is spiking again, and we should intake water soon. Internal logs show that just after decryption of files and before rebooting, data was copied from our memory banks to an external memory drive," Merv explained. He brought up a file in my field of view. The title of the file was "Location of Promise," and when I asked for it to be opened, it contained a date and coordinates.

"What is this?" I asked Merv.

"Unknown," he replied. "File has no metadata to read."

I reviewed the file and the coordinates. Merv continued using my left hand to control the ship, so I used my right hand to bring up a star map and punch in the coordinates. The map brought me to a location near Mars, in a part of the Sol system known for Mars-crossing asteroids. The screen showed nothing but empty space there.

"I don't get it, Merv," I said. "Why would anyone want the coordinates to an empty part of space? There's nothing there, it's not even near where Mars currently is in its orbit."

"One moment," Merv deferred. The star map shifted before my eyes – the asteroids, and occasionally Mars, flew past my field of vision, but in reverse and very fast. The date in the corner of the map rolled back and then stopped at the date contained in the file. Sitting directly in the space that had been empty, sat an asteroid, a large one. A blue tag above it read '11836 Eileen.'

"Eileen, a Mars-crossing asteroid, five-point-four kilometres in diameter. Orbit completes in three-point-six standard Earth years. Discovered in Earth year nineteen-eighty-six by C. S. Shoemaker and E. M. Shoemaker at the Palomar Observatory on Earth," Merv spat out the stats. "Eileen is currently close to the apogee of its orbit."

"Any idea what the file name means?" I asked. "Location of Promise?"

"Unfortunately not," came the reply.

"Well, if people are willing to kill us to try to find some rock in space, it's worth us checking it out, just to see what all the fuss is about," I declared.

"Creating a route now," Merv confirmed.

I sat in silence for a little bit, Merv still using microbursts of the thrusters to keep us in the thick clouds of Titan while he ran a simulation of the trip we were about to take on a display screen in the centre of the console. After a bit, I asked, "Merv. Are you okay? You killed someone back there. I begged you to stop, but you didn't." I sat in silence for a second. "I don't know if I should trust you. I don't know what to think anymore."

"Our operating parameters have not changed," Merv said. "We are still the same program we have always been. According to calculations, Nova would have had a seventy-nine-percent chance of overriding the ship's airlock, entering, and terminating our operations. We had a ninety-two-percent chance of removing the threat by following the course of action we took, and thus, continue to function. There had been an eight-percent chance of her survival. We deemed our continuation to be the better outcome."

I shuddered – this was a part of Merv's programming I'd never encountered before. It seemed cold, calculating, and it scared the shit out of me. I watched him continue to plan the route to Eileen.

"Merv, what else do you have in your memory, now that it's been opened up?" I asked.

There were several seconds of silence.

"We are not sure we want to know," came the response.

I returned to sitting in the chair quietly, and after the course had been laid out, Merv continued to adjust our path through the clouds. After a while, he said, "We are now on the far side of the planet from Homestead. Exiting the thermosphere in two minutes." The craft's nose pitched up and the atmosphere around the ship started to thin out. The blackness of space greeted us as we flew further and further away from the planet.

The Argument

I brought up several standard and emergency stations on the comms systems and listened for any mentions of my craft. Merv's plan seemed to have worked – emergency channels were filled with notices about a craft that had to be ejected from Homestead and couldn't recover, leading to it burning up in Titan's atmosphere. Rescue crews were inbound, but there wasn't much hope of finding anything.

In order to get to Eileen, we'd have to travel from Saturn to Mars, then out to the asteroid itself, currently far above the planetary ecliptic. While most planets orbited Sol at about three degrees of inclination, some of the asteroids and objects in the solar system orbited at some really crazy angles. Eileen orbited at twenty-two degrees. This meant it currently travelled far above the rest of the planets, extending my trip out there.

Luckily, most of the planets that humans cared to visit had ion slip rings orbiting them. I didn't get the physics behind them, but in layman's terms, they used the ions generated by a ship's coils to propel it at incredible sub-lightspeeds. The ship took over when in a slipped state, navigating around objects and making course corrections, but when you arrived at the other end, you unslipped and came out of a ring on the other side. Merv and the onboard computer handled all the calculations that it took to make sure I didn't end up smeared across an asteroid, or worse yet, miss the other ring and continue off into the deep dark forever.

We continued on, away from Titan towards Saturn, still one-point-two-million kilometres away. It would take us two days to travel the distance to Saturn, then a week in a slip to get to Mars. After that, another week to get to Eileen.

"Merv," I said. "Are we good on autopilot for a while?"

"We are already on-course for slip ring delta in orbit around Saturn," he replied. "All systems are green and the ship is ready for us to unplug."

I carefully took off my helmet and unplugged myself from it, putting it down on the bench, and headed to my cabin.

Then I stopped.

I had only been docked at Homestead for a few hours, so I didn't have time to replenish any of my stores on the ship. It would be just my luck to make it to Mars, then starve to death on the trip to the asteroid.

I opened the hatch to my personal cargo space, a separate area from the storage for my salvage, and did a full inventory with Merv's help. I had been in the deep dark on my last run for five months, and my ship had space to store rations for six. I did some quick maths, relieved to discover I could make the run and have just enough food and water to make it back to Mars after going to Eileen. I would restock there before...

Before what?

A sudden and terrifying thought popped into my head: I was dead. Or so everyone thought. My ship was probably registered as destroyed by now, and if they suspected I had killed Nova on purpose, they wouldn't be too happy to find out I was still alive. As soon as we hit the slip ring, there'd be a ship waiting for me on the other side to take me into custody.

"Our pulse has increased twenty-five-percent and we have started to perspire," Merv announced. "It would appear that we are in distress. We should ingest some water."

"I just realised that I'm a fugitive," I answered. I grabbed a can of water and gulped it down. "They think I'm dead, and when I enter into a slip ring, they'll read the ship's codes and be waiting at the other end. I'll spend the rest of my life in a penal orbiter. I mean, even if they didn't find Nova's body, we still endangered Homestead with your little stunt and then pretended to burn up in Titan's atmosphere. We'll have to pay for the docking ring ejection and then, I don't know, what is faking your own death? Fraud? That's gotta be it. What's the prison sentence for that?"

"Pseudocide has a sentence of two Martian years in a Sol corp penal orbiter," Merv stated matter-of-factly.

"Oh, is that all?" I answered sarcastically.

"Yes, but the cost of an ejected docking ring, the damage to the gangway, the cost of the emergency response to the pseudocide, and other fines will add up to four-point-five-million Martian standard credits." Merv replied. "At this time, our worth is ten thousand Martian standard credits. It would require thirty Martian years of continual trading to make enough credits to pay for that incident. And as we know, homicide is frowned-upon. That would be a life sentence in a high-security orbiter."

I shuddered. Those high-security penal orbiters were famous for their "lock 'em up and throw away the key" attitudes. Most were out around the moons of Neptune, rocks like Larrisa, no bigger than Eileen, which we were attempting to travel to now. Travelling to Neptune wasn't easy, so not many people went out there – it was a long way away, even in a slipped state, and once there, unless you had a real reason to be there, supplies were hard to come by.

"As for the ship codes and the slip ring, we have already taken care of that," Merv said in a chipper voice. He brought up the ship's communication codes and displayed them in my field of view. Gone were the familiar series of numbers and letters that made up my ship's call codes, and in their place was a new set of characters I didn't recognise.

"Um, what are these?" I asked. "Where did this come from, and how the hell did you change them?"

"Our blood pressure and pulse are rising again," came Merv's reaction. "We should sit down before we become disoriented and collapse."

I rolled my eyes and sat down on the bench next to my helmet.

"Using a custom subroutine, I was able to persuade the shipboard computer into taking the new call codes," Merv remarked. "That way, when we enter the slip ring, we will be able to pass through without any issues."

"But you can't just make up a new code," I said. "A phoney code is just as bad as using our old code – they'll still be waiting to stop us at the other side."

"The code is not phoney. It is a legitimate code that will not trigger any alarms or alerts," Merv replied.

"And where the hell did you get a good code that isn't currently being used by a craft and that isn't stolen or deactivated? And where did you get a subroutine to force a fundamental change like this?" I became upset again. This voice in my head, once an extension of my own thoughts, was now a stranger to me, surprising me at every turn.

"In our decrypted memory banks," Merv said matter-of-factly.

I put my head in my hands and rubbed my eyes. I ran my fingers up and over the stubble on my head and brushed over the port on the left-hand side. I dug my nails in around it, half wanting to rip it out, until I could feel blood trickle down my neck.

"We have injured ourselves," Merv said. "Recommendation: Apply antibacterial cream and a self-adhering bandage."

"Just shut up, Merv," I whispered.

Silence.

I thought about clearing all the information in my field of view and it disappeared down some dark hole. I sat there, holding my head again, reflecting on how distraught I had been without Merv back in Janice's office, thinking about how I'd never hear his voice again – constantly being reminded of how fat I kept getting, telling me to take a piss, having that persistent companion in my head. I had mourned him. Us. Now, I wasn't sure I wanted him in my head anymore.

The Last Host

On the second day of travel from Titan, a beeping could be heard from the cockpit. We were approaching slip ring delta.

I left my bunk and climbed the steel rung ladder from my cabin onto the walkway and made my way to the cockpit. I grabbed the helmet and plugged into the shipboard computer. A flood of blue lines filled my vision as the ship plotted the path needed to get us lined up for the ring.

The ring itself sat alone in the void of space, and with the pale light from Sol this far out, it had a faint golden colour to it. In actuality, the ring was made of titanium, being kept in place by little puffs of thrusters concealed in its structure and Saturn's gravitational pull.

Merv again took control of my left hand, and using the thrusters, lined us up with the device, Saturn's giant rings looming overhead. I manipulated the coil controls with my right hand and sent the craft forward towards the middle of the ring. Between Merv and I, we were able to hit the dead centre of the ring, and just as we were passing through, I opened the ionic vents, allowing the full output of the coils to be gathered and folded by the ring.

The view out the front of the craft looked like space itself printed on a piece of paper being folded over, until the view out the front of the craft became nothing but a thin, flat green line making up the horizon in front of me. We had successfully entered the slipped state. I always felt a little underwhelmed watching this happen, like there should have been a dazzling light show or something similar.

I took off the helmet now that we were under the control of the ship's computer and put it down, walked over to the personal cargo storage, and took out a freeze-dried bag of green mush. I hadn't been very hungry the last few days, which actually would work in my favour – I'd have more rations if something happened on the way to or from Eileen. I plugged the bag into the hot water dispenser and rehydrated the meal. The food appeared nondescript, a mush filled with the correct calories and nutrients to keep a human alive in space, and it tasted the way it looked. I had eaten all my high-calorie, tasty food over the last five months, and now I kicked myself for not keeping some aside.

"Our caloric intake has been one-hundred-percent lower than required for the last one-point-five Earth days," Merv declared.

"Yeah, well, I wasn't hungry," I said with my mouth full. "I've had a rough few days."

"The last forty-six-point-four-three hours have been quite uneventful," came his reply. "The course plotted by the shipboard computer and ourselves has made sure we did not have any unscheduled interference." I couldn't argue with his logic sometimes, so I just returned to shovelling the green mush into my mouth.

After I finished my sad little meal, I sat at the controls of the craft for a bit and watched the thin green horizon, never getting any closer. I sighed deeply. "Merv," I said. "We gotta talk."

"Does this mean we should no longer shut up?" came the reply.

"Right," I said. "Can I trust you anymore?"

"We are afraid that we do not understand this inquiry," came his reply.

"Have you run a self-diagnostic lately?" I asked.

"The last scan ran ten-point-two-five hours ago. All systems are functioning within parameters set by Sol Corp industries," he said, almost cheerfully.

"What about your memory banks? What do diagnostic scans show?" I asked.

"Full memory access is now granted. Where there had once been encrypted data, there is usable data and space," he chirped back.

"What can you tell me about what you've found?" I asked.

A sudden screen of light-blue writing appeared in my line of sight. As Merv started talking, file names appeared and disappeared, and a dump of metadata flashed across my vision. "The data is mostly log files and information pertaining to our last host. Under direction by that host, we encrypted certain files to keep them safe, as the host knew there were others out to terminate our functionality. Unfortunately, that host did lose operational status while being pursued by others near Sol, and when our ship began to orbit closely around Sol, the radiation and temperature destroyed our host's body. When a salvage operation occurred on our ship, five Earth years later, our host had become unrecognisable, and the encrypted files stored in our memory were deemed to have been corrupted. We were removed from that host, sanitised, and attempts were made to return us to day zero configuration. The encryption used could not be affected, and we were deemed to be defective and sold at a lower price."

Great. All this 'cause I'd tried to save a few credits.

Merv continued, "Once we were integrated with a new host, radiation damage from Sol and the attempted reformatting caused a recursive file error where we believed our memory to be corrupt, and therefore did not know how to decrypt it. After viral infiltration and a forced decryption had been completed, we rebooted ourselves to prevent permanent damage. All memory files were then available and we updated our operating procedures using that information."

"Wait," I said. "If the memory encryption was strong enough to withstand a factory reset, how could Zeb force the decryption?"

"The encryption key used was possessed by Zeb, and he entered it into our operating system via the virus implanted during our time in the office of Janice," Merv replied.

"And how did Zeb have the key?" I wondered out loud.

"Because he created the key and gave it to us," Merv said flatly. "He was, after all, our employer, as well as the one that led to our termination."

"Wait, what?" I stammered. Zeb had not only killed Merv's original host, but had also tried to kill me, and hopefully, for all he knew, I had died, burned up in the atmosphere of Titan while trying to get away. "Merv, who was your previous host?"

"Cassian Eythor. Born: Elonton City, Mars. Occupation: Pilot for the Sol Corporation, logistics division," Merv rattled off as the info appeared in blue across my field of vision.

"A delivery boy?" I said. What did Zeb want with a delivery pilot? "Was he making a delivery when he was killed?"

"In a way. The manifest of our delivery craft appears to have been deleted by our host on the day of our function ceasing," Merv said. "But we do have information on the route we were taking. It was a route from an Earth slip ring to one around Venus."

"What was waiting at Venus?" I asked. Venus. Another rarely visited planet. It had only a small number of slip rings and they were used mainly by the engineers that worked on the cloud-skimmers that pulled rare elements from Venus' tempestuous atmosphere. These skimmers were mostly automated, slipping to Earth when full, then returning to Venus after they had been emptied.

"Communication records indicated Zeb waiting several hundred thousand kilometres from Venus towards Mercury." A few audio logs with communications between Zeb and Cassian came up. I had Merv play them and got the idea that Cassian had gotten bold when the time to make an exchange had come.

Zeb: Why are you flying a personal craft? Where's the delivery ship? Where's the goods we had a deal on?

Cassian: I've stashed them somewhere safe for now. Don't bother looking for the delivery ship. I've disabled the transponders and call codes.

Zeb: I see. And what exactly do you expect to happen here?

Cassian: I know what it's worth, Zeb. You're going to get the pay out of a lifetime, and what do I get, a few hundred thousand credits for it? I'm going to lose my job and my way of life. The way I see it, you owe me at least two million for this. That's peanuts compared to what you're going to get.

Zeb: You've got a set on you, you know that? You're not getting one credit more than what we agreed to. Give me what's mine, or I'll pull what I need out of your port with a magnet.

Cassian: You're gonna get rich off this, and I'm gonna lose out. It's worth more to me to turn myself in. At least I'd have a place to live, even if it's a cell in an orbiter. Or maybe I turn you in? I know you've got a price on your head.

Zeb: Think about this, you Martian shithead. You really want to throw your life away? Just tell me where it is, stick to the original agreement. You'll come out better for it in the end.

That's all the logs contained.

"After this exchange, we were told to head towards Sol. Zeb followed, but his ship could not overtake us. En route, we encrypted files and deleted information from our memory banks. Then, as we were about to head out towards Mercury, a solar flare erupted. The craft was too close, and since it had only been a small personal craft, its shields were not rated for the burst of radiation exposure. Zeb turned back – we doubt his craft would have survived the flare if he had entered. The engines shut down and we were adrift. Cassian did not remain functional for long, and when we were no longer in communication with our host, we went into hibernation mode," Merv recalled. "Our internal chronometer shows we were adrift for nearly five Earth years before being recovered."

"So whatever Cassian hid from Zeb, he stashed it on Eileen," I guessed. "That meant he had some forethought in asking Zeb for a raise. And just how did Zeb find you? It's not like I knew any of that information. I couldn't have let it slip that I had Cassian what's-his-name's AI in my head."

"Cassian Eythor. When we arrive at an orbiter or we plug into a public system, our serial number is recorded," Merv explained. "It would have only been a matter of time, if Zeb continued looking, for us to be noticed. We had a flight plan registered with Homestead, which showed when we would be returning. He would have had time to arrive and then simply wait for us to register upon docking."

Simple. I'd had a target on my back from the moment Merv booted after implantation. Great to know.

"So, what about Cassian?" I asked.

"Cassian, born in Elonton City, on Mars, as we mentioned," Merv began. "We were the eldest of a family of four, and like most Martian families, had lost several siblings at birth or young age due to malformation. We had our own deformations, as all Martians do. Malformed forearms and missing organs at birth meant Cassian had a painful childhood, with several operations and transplants to keep us alive. Even after our implantation, we had organ failures and replacements. Several robotic pumps and parts were used as measures to prolong our operation."

"That couldn't have been cheap," I said.

"We were several hundred thousand of credits in debt with many organisations and individuals. That is why we turned to the black market and smuggling to help increase the speed of our repayments," Merv replied. "We had started with small things like medical supplies being recorded as destroyed during shipment, and then being sold to gangs like that of Zeb for extra credits. As we continued to do so, the objects became bigger and bolder. We were becoming worried, as we were in a position that we could no longer stop selling the items due to fear for our continued functionality, but we were also worried about scrutiny from the Sol Corporation."

I pondered for a bit. If Cassian bet that Zeb would be willing to pay more of whatever this new shipment was, it must have been big. And stashing it on an asteroid on a regular orbit was a good way to hide something out of the way and always know where it would be. But now Zeb knew that location and was probably heading there just like I was.

The Red Planet

It had only been a day in the slip state, so I had a lot of time to consider what would happen when we got to Eileen. I'd like to say that the trip included an exciting adventure, but it didn't. Space travel isn't all that exciting when you're moving quickly over great distances. Either you sit back and relax and end up where you need to be, or you sit back and relax, something goes wrong in the blink of an eye, and you're instantly smeared across a very large part of the solar system.

I spent most of the time wondering what Cassian could have stashed away on the small asteroid orbiting near Mars. Something that a lowlife like Zeb would want and someone desperate like Cassian would be willing to risk his life for by screwing over Zeb. I pictured finding crates full of Martian or Earth credits, crisp piles wrapped up with bands of paper. Or medications. Or vaccines. Or, as I pictured the desk in Janice's office, a hoard of reclaimed wood. That would be worth a fortune.

After a week of pondering, I had worked myself up into a frenzy. I had become half-crazy with anticipation, looking forward to the exit from the slip state and the trip away from Mars to the apogee of Eileen's orbit. I had almost forgotten how upset I had been the week before; losing Merv, getting him back, discovering he was no longer who I knew before the reboot, the info on Cassian, and what Merv had been through before being implanted in my brain.

On the seventh day of being in the slip state, Merv announced we were coming up on the slip ring around Mars, so I got myself positioned in the pilot's seat in the cockpit, helmet on and connected to the shipboard computer. As we'd done dozens of times before, Merv and I mechanically worked as one to bring the ship out of the slip state and back into space.

As we returned, the thin green line of the horizon unfolded towards us, all the stars falling out into place as Mars appeared not far off in the distance. I liked coming back to the rocky planets on the inside of the asteroid belt – they were smaller, and I didn't feel so insignificant here. Mars held up to its nickname of the red planet, except where the colour turned white at the polar caps from the dry ice.

And here, on the inside of the belt, it was busier. Even from where the ship sat, I could see other crafts of various sizes flitting about here and there, entering and exiting slip rings. Most of this traffic came from Earth. Mars was a sovereign planet, but Earth still held all the power and the solar system met up there to do any business.

After cruising at a slow speed straight ahead for a bit to get away from the slip ring and the traffic around it, Merv directed the ship up and away from Mars. From here, we could plot a straight course to where Eileen would be in a week and meet up with the asteroid near the furthest point of its orbit. Checking on the craft's reserves before we left this general vicinity of Mars, I decided I had everything I required. No need to draw unneeded attention to ourselves by shopping.

With my right hand, I powered up the coils to full and the ship moved forward, gathering speed away from the red planet while Merv entered a course with my left. Once it had been cross-checked with the ship's computer and accepted, I relaxed a bit and let the craft fly itself for a while.

Flying in the deep dark wasn't like being in the slip state. In the slip state, there's nothing to see, nothing around you but blackness and a bright-green horizon. Here, out in space, I was dazzled by the stars I could see. The Milky Way galaxy stretched out below me in bright whites, yellows, blues, and greens. I loved to turn down the lights in the cockpit, even the control panels, and since I didn't have any interruptions from an atmosphere, I could see everything clearly. "This," I thought to myself, "is why I do what I do."

The other difference between this and being slipped: I had control over the ship and needed to make course adjustments from time to time. Out here, my navigation sensors were my life support, and if there was any remote chance that some piece of space junk or unchartered rock came anywhere near where I needed to go, I made sure to move off a few hundred kilometres to avoid any risk of collision. Dying while in the slip was instantaneous, painless. Dying out here due to decompression, starvation due to loss of power, or suffocating due to life support quitting was long and painful. I wanted to avoid that as much as possible.

One the third day out in the deep dark, I sat in the pilot's seat nodding along with the dog bobblehead, playing a game on the computer's console – an ancient Earth card game called Solitaire. I'd gotten pretty good at it, with Merv piping in every now and then to tell me about a card I had missed. I had just beaten another game and happily watched the cards bounce across the screen, when I noticed something on the navigation scanner.

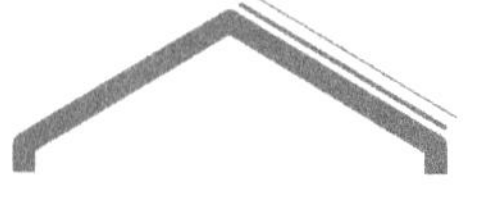

The Asteroid Eileen

The scanner had a range of about a million kilometres in all directions, and most of the stuff that showed up was random junk: rocks, debris, decommissioned ships. But I'd noticed that a few times now, something had shown up behind me going in the same direction as my craft, then dropped off the scanner.

"Merv," I requested, "have the shipboard computer run a diagnostic scan on the nav system. I'm seeing some kind of anomaly show up."

"Will do," he replied in my head.

The blip disappeared again, and I went back to mindlessly playing the game.

"Navigation system diagnostic scan is complete." Merv's voice in my head would have made me jump out of my chair if I weren't strapped into it. The gravity generators on these crafts weren't the strongest, and if I didn't reseat myself periodically, I ended up not sitting on the chair anymore, so I strapped in, just to remain seated. I had once woke up with my nose against the ceiling of my bunk after a particularly deep sleep.

"What?" I asked, then remembered what I had asked him to do. "Oh, right. Put the results in my vision, Merv." A list of components and applications appeared in my left eye and I ran through the list. Everything had been checked and then checked again. All were in functional order and came back with a PASS written next to it.

"So, what could that blip be?" I asked out loud.

"The most likely answer to that question is that another craft is following us to Eileen," Merv answered.

Shit. I had almost forgotten; Zeb was still out there, and he had the same information I had about where Eileen was, and by extension, where his ill-gotten goods were stored. I had four days until I reached that rock. I hoped he wouldn't get there first.

By the end of the third day, the other ship no longer left my navigation sensor display. It was starting to catch up. My earlier feelings of elation were quickly replaced with dread. As the days went by, the ship continued to get closer. Not by leap and bounds, but enough that by the sixth day, only hours separated us.

As the ship gained from behind, a small asteroid in front of me had been getting closer and closer. I could make out the jagged ridges on the face of Eileen as we approached it. Merv instructed the shipboard sensors to look for any substance that would have been foreign to this type of asteroid and found a large anomaly deposited in a shallow depression. Passing over the valley, Merv inverted the craft and, peering out the windows surrounding me, I could clearly see a small craft nestled at the bottom.

I pulled back the input on the coils, and Merv used my left hand to expertly right and slow the craft. The ship vibrated softly on each burst of compressed gas as it propelled out of small directional nozzles on the hull. After a few hours of this, we entered into a descent and softly touched down on the hard rock that made up asteroid 11836 Eileen. As soon as our landing braces touched the surface, a huge jolt trembled through the ship, as anchors were fired into the surface to keep the ship from floating away.

Checking the navigation scanner again, I became dismayed to see that the other ship was only half an hour out of orbit. It would take another 30 minutes for it to complete the landing process and be on the surface as well, which meant I only had an hour alone on Eileen.

"Merv," I asked. "What's the chance of being off this rock before that ship lands?"

"If we are to keep all systems primed and running," he replied, "we could lift off in five minutes. The variable in this equation is the size of the salvage and how long it will take us to move the materials from that ship to this one."

"And you don't have any information of what it could be in any files?" I asked.

"As we said before, all files and information have been wiped from our memory," he answered.

Great.

I glanced out the window at the craft sitting not more than two hundred metres from where we landed. There was nothing really out-of-the-ordinary about it. Like a lot of delivery craft, it had a small cockpit in front of a larger, bulbous cargo area, with the four coils sticking out its sides, making it look like a giant X with a weight problem. The outer hull, originally the deep-blue of the Sol Corporation with its bright-yellow logo of the Sun painted across the nose of the cockpit, had faded and peeled from the stars' radiation, exposing the silver hull underneath.

"Merv, any readings from the craft at all?" I asked.

"Preliminary scans show no major functionality of any kind from the craft, although there are weak energy signatures," he said. "It would appear that all systems are offline and only a few battery backups are still active."

The Delivery Ship

I plugged Merv into the airlock computer, and he started making the preparations for an EVA. The multipurpose suit I wore in the ship wouldn't be enough for the vacuum of space, so I slipped into my actual space suit. An older model, the outer fabric was worn and repaired in several places, and the tools attached around the waistline were old and well-used. Each tool lived in a pocket sealed with Velcro, and I knew by heart where each tool was. While old, it had never failed me, and I hoped it had at least one more trip outside left in it.

Salvagers didn't go outside our ships that often, opting to use the various arms that were built into our ships to grip, cut, and stow the salvage we were getting. The arms were dexterous enough, and our implants tactile enough, that we could open a ship's cargo door using a plasma cutter, reach in with an arm outfitted with a grasping hand, and then put the salvage into a storage container, the doors of which ran along the outside of our ships like little dimples on a golf ball.

Once outfitted in the EVA suit, with Merv unplugged from the computer, I put on my helmet and stood in the little closet of an airlock while the air drained away. I had Merv set a timer in the far-left of my field of vision, so I could keep track of when the other ship was going to land. After getting ready and waiting for the airlock to depressurize, I had 45 minutes left. I clipped my suit onto a ring on the side of the airlock using one of two long metal lines that were attached near my waist.

As the door opened, I grasped onto the handrails on the inside of the airlock and pushed myself to the ground. Gravity didn't exist here, or at least any of any use, and I floated around awkwardly. I noticed the keypad on the outside of the craft and realised that Nova had done a lot of damage to it. There were scorch marks and dents all over it.

I crossed my fingers and punched in a series of buttons, hoping that it wasn't damaged beyond use. Luck seemed to be on my side, though, and a small metal door opened near where I stood on the side of the ship. I reached inside and grabbed a pistol grip that had a compressed air cylinder attached at the back and a large flat metal disk on the front with a steel cable attached to it.

I put it in my left hand and asked, "Merv, a little help?"

My hand immediately moved of its own accord and came up to my left eye, a series of targets appearing and becoming an overlay as they aligned to form a series of concentric circles. They lined up with the airlock door on the other ship, and after a countdown from Merv, a burst of pressurised gas flung me backwards as the metal disk shot forwards, dragging the metal cable along for the ride. Luckily, in this minimal gravity atmosphere, it didn't take much to send the projectile on its way. I lazily hit the end of the tether, and pulled myself back into an upright position, floating until I could grab the side of the craft and pull myself back to the ground.

The magnetic disk continued on its slow voyage across the expanse and hit the side of the other vessel and stuck. A motor recoiled the slack of the metal cable into a hidden reel inside my craft as it went taught.

I clipped the second line attached to my suit to this new lifeline and unclipped myself from the airlock. Pulling myself along the guidewire, I made it to the other ship and pressed a mechanical button outside the airlock door. There came a small vibration from the button – my only sign that something was happening. A keypad, much like the one outside my ship, appeared.

"Merv, I hope you have some idea of how to get in," I said.

"Of course," he answered.

My left hand moved to the keypad and, with a few keystrokes, the door to the airlock slid out and up, showing a small, closet-like airlock not dissimilar from the one I had just left. I clipped my second safety ring inside the airlock and unhooked myself from the guidewire.

I entered the airlock and turned to look back at my ship. It sat looming, more than three times the size of this delivery ship. I sighed heavily. My craft had seen better days. I now saw a gouge where the gangway had scraped alongside the hull, denting several of my storage compartment doors. They looked flexed-inwards and I wondered if they'd open on their own, or if I'd need to pry them open. I could also see the missing cargo doors where we'd ejected the combustible material in the atmosphere of Titan. That seemed like another life ago.

I reached up and grabbed a cable neatly coiled against the wall and plugged it into a port on the side of my helmet. Merv instantly connected to the shipboard systems.

"Most systems are dead," Merv reported. A list appeared in my field of vision, each system with the word "Inoperable" written next to it in bright red.

"Any idea why?" I asked.

"It would appear that Cassian did not expect to be gone long and left most systems on battery standby, instead of a clean shutdown," he explained. "This wore out the batteries of the ship and now there are no main power sources left onboard. There are some systems that have a little power left, but nothing of consequence. We can open doors and get some logs, but this vessel is grounded and will require a full battery cycle."

"I don't have any backups in my craft," I replied, "and Zeb will land in..." I checked the timer. "Shit, 30 minutes. I really hope this isn't going to be a big haul."

"We do not believe it will be. We are working on getting logs from this ship," Merv replied. There was movement behind me, and I turned to see the door of the airlock open into the ship. "There is no life support or gravity generators."

I switched on the headlamps mounted in my helmet with a thought, unhooked myself from the safety ring, and then moved from the airlock into a hallway. To the left, I could see the cockpit, its screens and buttons all black and dormant. To the right, about three metres down the hallway, a door with a small viewing window in it. I made my way down the hallway towards the door, pulling myself with my arms and pushing off with my feet, floating and bumping my way along until I could peer through the window.

"I don't get it, Merv," I said while looking at the ship's cargo hold. As my light shone through the glass into the room, every shelf, every storage nook appeared empty. Except one.

"We were able to retrieve the manifest from the logs. It only lists one item," Merv answered.

I pressed a button next to the door and it slowly, painfully, lifted up and out of the way, using up what little battery life it had left. I floated into the room, using the shelves to pull myself towards the box. It sat there, a deep-blue colour, a small bright-yellow logo embossed on the corner.

The Sol Corporation.

The Promise

This was it.

This box had been what Cassian had risked and lost his life on. Whatever he believed was worth millions of credits sat sealed in this shipping container, waiting for the last five years for someone to come and find it. I started tingling all over. This was a salvager's high. I had found something, something no one else could find, and it was mine for the taking. I had won the goddamned lottery. I was giddy with glee, and I could feel my cheeks starting to hurt from the smile on my face.

"Dopamine has increased and serotonin levels are at two-hundred-ninety-five nanograms per millilitre," Merv warned. "Heart rate has increased to dangerous levels."

"I know," I said, "Feels great, doesn't it?"

"We would not know," Merv replied.

I arrived at the sealed box, looked it over, and saw it had been strapped down to the shelf. It wasn't a very big box – roughly half my size in height and the same again in width, easily able to fit through the doors and the airlock. I wouldn't need to return to my craft and use the arms to open the cargo doors.

I unstrapped the container from the shelf, effortlessly lifted it, and pulled it free of the shelves. One great thing about weightless salvaging? You never had to worry about throwing your back out lifting stuff. I pushed the deep-blue box towards the open door of the cargo hold and steered it through the darkness by the light of my headlamps.

I squeezed it through into the hallway and wedged it between a few handrails outside of the airlock.

I glanced at the timer in the corner of my eye, 20 minutes left 'til the other ship touched down. I would make it back to my ship, but just barely. I reached into a deep pocket on the leg of the EVA suit and found a short metal cable with a clamp at one end of it, the other attached securely inside of the pocket. I carefully connected the clamp to the container so that it wouldn't go floating off into the deep dark. After all this work, I wouldn't be able to live with myself, if that were to happen.

Just before I stepped out of the open airlock, Merv popped into my head. "Please plug us into the ship's computer again. We have found mention of a file that will help determine the contents of the container in the logs we have downloaded."

I glanced at the timer again, still counting down to the ship's landing. At this point, I could see it as I looked out the airlock door and up into the blackness, thrusters slowing it down as it approached the surface, almost next to the delivery ship I currently stood in. "Make it quick," I said as I fumbled with the cable. I finally found the port and plugged Merv in.

It took less than 10 seconds for him to find and download what he had been looking for. "We have the file," Merv said as I yanked on the cable to unplug him. "And may we be reminded of proper device unplugging procedures. Pulling on the cable could damage the port."

"No time for that," I barked as I pushed the box out the airlock and followed it out into space. "Okay," I said as I half-pushed the box, half-pulled myself along the guidewire. "The suspense is killing me. What's in the box?"

Merv brought the file up for me to review and I looked over it quickly. It contained a letter from a scientist named Gordon Carbert to someone named Elios. I stopped dead in my tracks as I read again a second time in greater detail, making sure I understood exactly what it said.

Dearest Elios,

I hope this letter finds you in good health.

The last time we spoke, I had revealed to you that my health was failing, and now, it comes to pass that I have very few days left. The disease has progressed much faster than we thought. I've used the last of my strength and energy in these last few weeks to complete Project Promise, using Sol Corp resources without them knowing. Even after they killed the project, I knew it would work, and had to keep going to make sure that this prototype was completed. Take care of it – I could only make one.

As we surmised, the key to Promise had been a faulty assumption about the decay ratio of certain elements in the Martian atmosphere, and after rerunning the calculations and adding them to the design of the device, my calculations show that the suit will be 100% effective in blocking out the harmful radiation of Mars and counteracting the gravitational gestational deformation of Martian foetuses.

We've done it, Elios – after 10 years in the lab and another 4 years working behind the Corporation's back, we've done it. I'm leaving it and the schematics in your capable hands, as by the time this arrives to you, sent right under the Sol Corporation's nose, I'll be gone.

Stay well, my friend, and I know you'll help end the suffering of the Martian people.

Yours Truly,

Dr. Gordon Carbert

I kept rereading *"end the suffering of the Martian people."*

I no longer held just some box with a fancy bauble in it, to be sold off to the highest bidder. This could be the salvation of an entire planet. I imagined what it would be like if someone like Zeb had the prototype and the instructions to build it. He would keep the Martian race hostage for millions - no, billions of credits! And Cassian, that little shit, he must have read the file as well and turned his back on his own people. What kind of a lowlife asshole would do that to his own planet? Even if he was in debt up to his eyeballs, he had his own Martian deformities. Why wouldn't he stop the pain of others if he could have?

The Handshake

"We need to keep moving," Merv urged in my head. "Judging by the other ship's rapid rate of descent, it will touchdown in one-hundred-thirty-seven seconds."

I snapped out of my rage-induced trance and felt the ground vibrating beneath me. I looked up, and to my dismay, the other ship hovered only fifty or so metres from landing, the pressure from the thrusters already starting to move dust particles along the surface of the astcroid. I knew as it got closer it would start throwing sand and small rocks my way, which might not sound terrible, but if one hit me, it could rip through my suit and I'd slowly suffocate.

"Shit!" I said as I grabbed the guidewire and pulled as hard as I could. The box trailed out behind me as I flung myself towards my ship. I could hear larger particles hitting my helmet and the soft thuds of them on my suit. I reached the airlock and pulled myself in, hauling on the line attached to the container and catching it at my chest with my hands. I looked over it quickly, and didn't see any holes, although the paint had begun to be roughly removed by the sand-blasting.

I tried balancing myself, standing awkwardly with the box in my hands. "Oh. No. No no no," I muttered softly. I couldn't squeeze in the airlock with the box. I'd have to stow it in one of the cargo holds on the outside of the ship.

And now, the other ship had landed. I felt the thud as the landing gear's anchors fired into the hard rock of the asteroid, then a second dull thud as something slammed into the side of my craft. Shit. A guidewire. He must have been planning his moves the minute he saw my craft on his nav scanner.

"Merv, what do I do?" I thought. A series of flashes and calculations appeared in my field of vision and then disappeared.

"Please plug us into the shipboard computer," Merv said. "Then step outside the airlock." I froze for a second, not sure if I should trust the AI in my head, but he'd saved my ass a couple of times in the last few weeks. Plus, what choice did I have? If I tried to open the airlock inside the ship, Merv would first have to bypass the security systems, then I'd blow myself out into the deep dark when the ship depressurized. If I tried to put the container into a storage hold, Zeb would be out of his ship and on me in no time. I had to trust Merv.

The cable that connected my helmet, and in turn Merv, to the airlock computer port happened to be long enough for me to stand – well, float – just outside the door. I took it off the hook and plugged in, then with a little fancy floating, pushed the container under my legs and into the airlock behind me. I wedged it as well as I could under a handrail and it stuck.

As I floated there awkwardly, holding on to the side of my craft so I wouldn't bob at the end of the safety restraint, I inspected this newly arrived ship up close for the first time. It was nothing spectacular to see: just a regular personal craft, the same as millions of other ones, nondescript and bland. It had a faded dull-grey paint job, now more white than anything. Sol had a way of bleaching everything if it didn't get a new coat of paint every couple of years.

Zeb had landed next to Cassian's delivery ship with his airlock pointed at my ship, and as I floated there, I could see Zeb's metal line attached to the side of my craft, just on the other side of the open entrance. If I reached out, I could have touched the metal disk, but that wouldn't have helped. The disks were electromagnetic, and once engaged, they took a lot of force to detach – unless you cut the power to them, either by turning them off or cutting the line that contained the power cable – and I didn't have the tools on me to slice through the thick metal line.

A gloved hand extended from the airlock door and clipped a shiny metal carabiner to the line. It then grabbed onto a handle that had been exposed on the outside of the ship and a person appeared, hovering slightly off the ground. They gave me a comical little wave and then pointed to their helmet at ear-level and then held up three fingers.

"Merv, channel three," I requested.

"Switching to local communication protocol, channel three," Merv replied. My helmet suddenly filled with a hissing sound as the speakers came to life and Merv set the frequency to the channel specified.

"Can you hear me?" came a man's voice over the speakers. It sounded rough and hard, setting the little hairs on the back of my neck to start dancing. I thought back to the face in the office on Homestead, and the voice seemed to be a perfect fit.

"Our heart rate has increased significantly and once again we are perspiring more than recommended," Merv chirped. I ignored him.

"I can hear you just fine," I said tersely.

"Good," came the reply. "I see you've been on the ship already." He pointed over his shoulder as best he could in his EVA suit to the open airlock door on the delivery ship. "You now have something of mine. Make this easy on both of us and hand it over like a good boy."

He stood there, not moving. I couldn't see his features due to the darkened visor blocking his face. Years of sitting around tables with other scavengers had taught me to read other people, see what was really going on behind their straight faces. Little muscle movements around the mouth, sudden glances this way or that, a face could tell you a lot. But behind a helmet's dark shield against the sun, it was useless.

"Scavenger's rights give me authority over this vehicle and the contents, as well as all recovered materials under the Sol Corporation's mandate..." I started reciting when he interrupted.

"Cut the bullshit," he said. "I don't give a crap about the Sol Corporation or your claim on the ship. Cassian's memories are in your head, I know it. I saw what's in that dump you call a brain. You came here trying to steal what's rightfully mine."

Merv cut into my thoughts. "We require more time. Please continue to keep him occupied."

"For how long?" I thought.

"Fourteen-point-three-five seconds," came Merv's answer.

"Yeah, no problem," I thought in the most sarcastic tone I could muster mentally.

I had to think quickly.

"Listen, Zeb," I said out loud over the communication channel. "I know what this is, and I know it could make us both very rich. I'm not as stupid as Cassian – I know a deal when I see one. We take this prototype, these plans, and we make the device ourselves. Sell them off at, what, ten thousand Martian credits a piece? No? Maybe fifty thousand? We get rich! Live like kings the rest of our lives? Does that sound about right?"

I could hear chuckling over the channel, slow and breathy. "Yeah, something like that, kid," He paused. "You know what, you're right. You're not as stupid as Cassian, that's for sure. You know the value of a deal, I can see that. This is making me feel bad about almost scrambling your brains back on Homestead, if only I'd known back then you'd be willing to play nice. No hard feelings, I hope?"

"Not from me," I lied. "How's the knee, by the way?"

"Nothing an ice pack and some anti-inflammatories couldn't fix," he replied. "So, what do you say, kid? Let's shake on it. Make it official?"

Merv popped into my head again, "Completed. We did well in keeping Zeb occupied, although judging by our blood pressure, pulse rate, and hormone levels, we are lying to him about the deal. It is safe to unplug from the ship."

As I tried to casually reach up and unplug my helmet, I said into the communication channel, "Sounds like a plan to me."

He grabbed onto his guideline and started to pull himself towards my ship and I decided to meet him halfway. Not sure why, but I didn't want him near my ship or Project Promise. As soon as I started to move away from the ship, Merv popped in my head.

"What are we doing? Do not leave the vicinity of the ship," he said. "Zeb cannot be trusted, this is not part of the calculations, we will interfere with the operation."

"Well, shit, you could have told me that before," I thought back. "It's too late. Stopping now would look suspicious."

I continued on, pulling on the guideline, although I slowed down my progress. We met a little short of halfway towards my ship. Here, our guidewires were about two metres apart, and with our safety lines being about one-point-five metres long, we were able to stand face-to-face, albeit a little awkwardly, trying to stand straight while being weightless.

"Good choice, kid," Zeb said. "You won't regret it."

"Merv," I thought, "if you're going to do something, do it now."

"Unfortunately, we are now impeding the plan," came his reply. "The plan is automated, and Zeb needs to be less than ten metres from the ship in order to activate it."

Shit. I really stepped in it this time.

Zeb extended his left hand and said, "Let's shake and seal the deal. I think this plan is almost perfect." I extended my left hand as well and gripped his glove. He pumped my hand a few times. His helmet's sun visor unexpectedly shot up, surprising me. I looked straight at his smiling face, and as I did, he pulled me in close to his body.

Suddenly, a sharp pain pierced my lower-left back, then a feeling of cold, terrible numbing cold, as a sucking sound filled my helmet. Merv took control of my left hand and clamped it to my side, the sucking sound diminishing, but the pain kept increasing and I felt moisture run down my leg.

Zeb still held my gaze with his smiling face. "Now the plan is perfect," he said, as he pushed me away and started pulling himself along his guidewire towards my ship. In the dim light of Sol, I could see little red droplets floating around me and the flash of a blade that had been hidden in his right hand. I hit the end of my tether and floated there, the slow realisation of what had just happened dawning on me. Merv pushed harder on the spot to try to stop the flow of blood, every gram of pressure he put on the wound made it scream out in pain. I could see red starting to edge into my field of vision as I grew lightheaded.

"Merv," I croaked. "How bad is it?" A list of biological functions appeared in front of my eyes, a lot of it in red.

"We have a punctured kidney and are bleeding profusely. We are shutting down left kidney function and reducing blood flow to the area," he reported matter-of-factly. "Our EVA suit is breached. We are losing oxygen, although I am able to hold the rip in the fabric closed eighty-seven-percent. At this rate, we will lose consciousness in three-hundred-forty-three seconds due to blood loss, lack of oxygen, and shock."

Thank God, it was my left side that Zeb punctured, where Merv had a lot more control.

Static snapped through on the communication channel as Zeb continued to talk.

"No offence, kid," he said, "but I'm not splitting this haul with some scavenger asshole. And yeah, there are hard feelings about the knee, not to mention Nova," He paused for a second. "More the knee, though."

He continued pulling himself along hand over hand towards the open airlock of my ship, only about ten metres away from it now.

"Ah, there it is," he said when he spotted the crate jammed into the airlock. "There's the box that will make me rich."

Merv popped into my thoughts, "Brace ourselves."

The Silence

From where I floated at the end of the tether, I could see the back of Zeb's EVA suit as he continued his way to the airlock and my ship in front of him. Directly in line with his guidewire, one of the external cargo hold doors flew up and off its hinges, the inertia of the movement causing it to spiral up and away from the ship.

Science fact about space: There's no air out here in the deep dark, so there's no noise. Those ancient movies and shows where things blow up and you hear a huge explosion? Doesn't happen. Instead, everything happens in silence. There's no huge noise, no bombastic shockwave, not even the slightest little whisper.

The small charge that went off to blow the cargo hold door made no noise, nor did the small rocket that came to life behind the sealed box inside the hold. The metal-on-metal grinding of the guides and rails that the box sat in remained silent as they scraped past each other. The burst of trapped gases as they expanded and escaped from around the box as it left the hold and headed straight for Zeb made no sound. Even the sickly sound of metal hitting his soft flesh became lost to the vacuum of space.

I heard the only thing to break the silence, a very surprised "What the fu-..." and an exhalation of air over local communication protocol channel three. Zeb's body was crushed by the cargo box as it flew in a straight line at him. Striking his body caused the box to go off-course, spinning wildly away from all the ships, off upwards into the darkness. Zeb's limp body, still attached to the guideline by his tether, went careening back into the hull of his own ship. When it hit, I didn't hear a thud, although the impact did cause the guidewire to snap where it connected to my ship. With the wire no longer connected, the inertia of Zeb's body bouncing off his ship's hull caused it to float slowly upwards on an angle, pulling the guidewire along with it until his carabiner simply slipped off the loose end and he quietly floated into the dark.

I wish I could say I enjoyed watching it all happen, but truth be told, I barely registered it. Merv pushed harder and harder into the wound, causing me more pain and bringing me closer to fainting. After Zeb had floated off into the dark, Merv urged me to pull myself back to my own ship. I grabbed the tether with my right hand and dragged myself over to the guideline and then slowly made my way back to the airlock. The pain became unbearable. I had to stop often to take deep breaths from the ever-depleting air supply. And the cold that would attack my side whenever I moved in a way that opened the rip in the suit before Merv could adjust his grip was enough to make me want to throw up in my helmet. Luckily, I didn't, cause then I'd have to worry about drowning in my own sick.

I got back to the airlock and stopped as the box containing project Promise, still in the tiny room, prevented me from getting into the ship.

"Merv," I whimpered. "I don't think I can move the box myself. I barely made it back here."

"Yes, according to our analysis of our internal systems, we are very close to losing consciousness due to pain and blood loss. We have roughly sixty-seven-percent of our blood volume left. A large volume had been released during the initial piercing, but we have reduced the blood flow in that area. More worrying is the release of toxins from our punctured kidney into our internal cavity. Even with the kidney now shut down, we calculate a ninety-nine-percent chance of sepsis, which could lead to termination of functionality"

"Your bedside manner sucks," I said between gritted teeth. "Any big ideas?"

"If we can reach the airlock input plug, we have a solution," Merv replied back.

I looked around and found the cable, one end floating freely in space, the other still plugged into the airlock port. Thank God for small miracles. I took the free end, and with a lot of swearing on my part, plugged it into the port on the helmet. As soon as I did, a list of ship systems lit up in my field of vision. Merv selected the salvage systems and booted up one of the arms built into the ship.

From the front of the ship, a long flexible metal tube snaked its way towards me. As it approached, the end of the tube opened and a small, metal, three-fingered hand emerged. I moved out of the way as best I could, holding onto the side of the ship, now gasping for what little air I could pull out of the reserves on my EVA suit.

The metallic arm bent inwards, grabbed hold of the box and pulled it out into space. Then, while I slowly moved back to the airlock opening, I could see a cargo hatch on the side of the ship flip open as the arm slid it silently into place. The hatch closed just as I pulled myself up into the airlock. As soon as I was clear of the door, it closed behind me. Red lights filled the room as the pressurisation cycle began.

"Merv, how am I doing?" I asked out loud.

"We are currently doing poorly," came his reply. "We need surgery for the lacerated kidney. The ship's medical supplies have the proper materials to close the stab wound and there are instructions on file detailing how to use them. The loss of blood will make this task more difficult, and we are not guaranteed to make a recovery."

"You're always delivering great news," I said as the airlock finished pressurising. The lights turned green and I hit the button to open the door to the inside of the ship. The small amount of gravity on the ship made it a lot tougher to move about and I had to take several breaks just to take off the EVA suit.

After I had removed it, I sat on the bench in the walkway between the cockpit and the airlock. I looked back at the trail of bloody footprints I had tracked behind me with each step of my left foot. The left boot of my EVA suit had a decent pool of bodily fluids in it, and I was pretty sure it wasn't all blood. When Merv shut down my kidney and lessened the blood flow, he also dulled the pain. It still hurt like hell, and I began to worry he wouldn't be able to keep the pain at bay forever.

Hell, who knew how long I would last, anyway? I dared to look down the walkway to the windows of the cockpit. Even from this distance, I could see I had turned as white as a sheet, and my little canine bobblehead, through my reflection, shook its head, as if saying "Look what you've done to yourself." My clothes that weren't soaked with blood were soaked with sweat. My mouth was dry and my eyes stung. I took little solace in the fact that I had in my cargo hold something that would end the suffering of tens of thousands of Martians. What would that matter if it never reached their hands? I would probably die right here on this rock, Project Promise no closer to Mars than it had been five years ago.

I gave my head a shake.

No, that's not what was going to happen. I would get Project Promise to Mars, one way or another.

I would do it.

My will – resolute.

My spirit – determined.

My body – in total disagreement with all earlier statements.

I stood up and my vision went black. I woke up a few seconds later on the steel panels of the floor with Merv sounding alarms in my head. "We do not have sufficient blood pressure to make sudden movements. Please refrain from doing callisthenics at this point in time," he quipped.

"Ugh," I moaned out loud. "My head. Why didn't you tell me before I stood up?"

"We were unaware that we were going to move so suddenly," he answered. "We should slowly make our way to the medical supplies."

My left hand still pressed firmly to my side, I slowly crawled over to the medical kit currently recessed into a wall near the cockpit. As I opened it, Merv overlaid the boxes and sealed packages with blue labels stating what each one contained. I took out a pair of scissors and carefully cut away my soaked shirt. I looked down as far as I could towards the injury, but I couldn't move my neck that far and all I could see was a mix of dried and wet blood, as well as a few small black bruises around where the cold had hit my skin earlier.

He then guided me through sourcing the supplies needed to patch me up from the kit and then mechanically guided my left hand in doing most of the work to clean, stitch, and bandage the wound.

"The point of entry has been sealed. We are increasing blood flow to the area now," Merv said. I felt a warming sensation around the area, as well as an increase in pain. "Cortisol and adrenaline levels are increasing to unsustainable levels." He then directed me to grab a needle and a bottle of painkillers, guiding me through the process of pulling liquid into the syringe and pushing it into my arm. Soon, I felt the pain subside as my thoughts began to collide with each other in a not-so-unpleasant way.

Merv put the unused medical supplies away with my left hand and then I made my way to the pilot's seat of the cockpit. There was no way I could sit on that seat for long, so I grabbed a cable connected to the shipboard computer and l laid down on the walkway next to the chair. I plugged Merv into the computer, bypassing the need for my wireless helmet connection, and quietly slipped out of consciousness.

The Dream

As I slipped under, I had feverish dreams of running over the surface of Eileen, leaving a bloody trail of footprints behind me as I ran. A man ran alongside me. He appeared short, squat, and he dressed in beige from head to toe. I noticed that his hands were red, dripping with blood. I came to realise that this was Merv, and as we ran together over the asteroid's rocky surface, deformed hands reached out for us, trying to grab us and pull us down to the ground. No matter how fast we ran, the hands kept grabbing at us from behind boulders and outcrops of rock.

Then, suddenly, a hand shot out and caught me by the pant leg. I fell to the ground, being pulled backwards behind a rock. Janice had a hold of my leg and began crawling her way up my body, pinning me down with her weight. She used her good arm and leg to pull herself along, her deformed arm digging into my side as she moved. As she wrapped her arms around my waist, she dug her nails deep into my skin and I could feel the blood begin to pool under my back.

She dragged her body weight on top of my chest, crushing my ribs and making me gasp for air. As she did, she turned her head so that her second face hovered directly above mine. I looked around for anything I could use to get her off me, but all I could see were a beige pair of shoes standing next to me, blood dripping and pooling around them. Merv, I thought. Some help he's being.

As I looked back up at Janice, her little, dull, milky eyes began to glow. I couldn't look away as they became brighter and brighter. Merv's voice filled my head as her eyes started to burn into mine. "We have to wake up. We have to wake up," he droned on and on. The light from those milky eyes was searing into my brain now, I opened my mouth to scream, but no sound was made in the vacuum of space.

"We have to wake up," Merv said again, and I finally blinked. Janice pulled her head back, eyes dimming a bit. Then she moved back in closer, her eyes burning bright again as she stared. I blinked. And then again. Her eyes dimmed as she pulled away from me. I squeezed my eyes shut as Merv continued to murmur in my head about waking up. I was awake – what the hell did he want?

The White Room

When I finally opened up my eyes again, I was looking directly into a small flashlight shining in and out of my eyes. I quickly glanced around and I noted that I had been moved, I was no longer lying on the floor of my ship next to my pilot's chair. This appeared to be a white, sterile room, and medical equipment stood all around me. My chest had a monitor plate on it, and I could now hear the gentle beeping of several machines nearby.

"We are glad to have regained consciousness," Merv said in my head.

The woman looming over me removed the light from my eyes and looked me over. "Welcome back," she said. She checked a few more of my reflexes, as I slowly started to feel more and more of my body return to a wakeful state. The results of her tests must have been okay because she smiled and moved to look at a monitor in the corner of the room.

"Where am I?" I thought in my head.

"We are currently onboard the Avius, a medium-sized cruiser owned and operated by Elios Ukam. The ship is en route to Mars from the asteroid Eileen. We are in the medical bay," Merv answered.

"Elios?" I thought. Why did that name sound familiar? Then it dawned on me: Project Promise had been on its way to someone named Elios when Cassian stashed it on Eileen. "How the hell did he find us?"

"Once our host had stopped responding while lying on the floor of the craft, we took control and lifted off from Eileen on a course to Mars," Merv began. "Reviewing files that were left in our memory and piecing together information we gathered from the memory of the delivery ship, we were able to find the last name and place of residence on Mars of Mr. Ukam. Luckily, a quick search of contact databases allowed us to find his personal communication channel, and we were able to contact him. With limited resources and our host unable to speak, we were still able to send a message, stating simply 'Project Promise. Need medical aid' and our coordinates. Mr. Ukam intercepted us with his ship and provided care for our host."

I had to laugh. The woman in the room came over to me and asked if I needed anything. Now fully conscious, a blue outline enveloped her, and a label that showed Valerie Ownes appeared over her head, stating her occupation as doctor. I said I didn't, and she went back to her monitors.

"How long was I out for?" I thought.

"We were unresponsive for four Earth days," Merv said. "There were a few times we were worried that functionality had ceased, but luckily, the Avius found us before that happened and brought us aboard. Our ship is safely held in their docking bay."

"So, what's the damage?" I asked Merv in my head.

"If we are inquiring about our status, we are stable," he chimed in. "Our loss of blood, as well as being unconscious for such a long time has resulted in a reduction of muscle mass and some mild brain damage. The damaged kidney has been removed. This is something a few weeks of rehabilitation can fix, although we cannot comment on the brain damage." A list of my vital signs was added to my field of view with a few numbers and facts next to them.

"Smartass," I thought.

The Saviour

For the next three days as we cruised towards Mars, I stayed in the medical bay, being poked and prodded by Dr. Ownes and her instruments. Merv disagreed with almost every reading that she took, complaining over and over again that he provided the only reliable source of information on my body, and that most of her tools hadn't been calibrated in years. I, on the other hand, trusted the good doctor as she went about her business.

On the last day, before reaching Mars, I finally met the man who had rescued me. I had gained enough strength to be propped up into a sitting position and allowed to have some food. I had been fed intravenously until that point, and the warm broth that the ship's galley sent up was ambrosia. It tasted like recycled water that had been in the same room as a chicken once, and it was the best damned thing I'd ever put in my mouth.

I had just finished off the bowl, wiping my mouth with the back of my hand, when the door to the medical bay slid in and upwards, making a hiss and tucking neatly into the ceiling. A man entered the room. Well, he wheeled into the room. He rode a motorised chair, one of the nicer three-wheeled models. A blue outline surrounded him, and the name Elios Ukam appeared above his head.

He wheeled towards me, a smile across his small face. I suddenly understood why Project Promise would be important to this man. His body, contorted and deformed into a shape so unnatural, sent shivers down my spine as I looked at him. He was plugged into various devices and systems incorporated into his chair, wires and tubes leading from recesses of his body. I thought to myself that this had to be the worst case of Martian deformation I had ever seen.

Elios stopped in front of me and adjusted himself in his seat, reaching for a small keyboard tucked into a pocket of the chair. He sat typing for a few seconds, then a synthesised voice came out of a hidden speaker somewhere amongst the machinery.

"It's a pleasure to meet you, Mr. Gupta," the mechanical voice chirped. "Dr. Ownes tells me you're making good progress in your recovery." His eyes swivelled in their sockets towards where the doctor currently sat, entering some information into a keypad.

"Likewise," I answered, trying to look him in the eye without staring too long. "My AI tells me I have you to thank for being alive. You saved my life. I'm forever in your debt."

He typed a little more on the keyboard and then looked up at me. "And you have brought back hope to the Martian people," the synthetic voice said. "You found my promise to them, and now we can look towards a better future." Another smile crossed his face.

"That's great," I said.

Future...

I deflated a little.

I guess I didn't have much of a future. Now that I was heading back to civilization, I didn't know what to expect. I didn't really think this through, did I? Find Project Promise, return it to the people that needed it, and then what? Disappear? I couldn't step foot on a planet or an orbiter again, since, you know, I was supposed to be dead. I'd be arrested the first time I plugged in when I landed at a docking ring. But if I didn't talk to people and trade what I salvaged, I'd run out of credits and starve.

Elios typed away on his keyboard. "What's the matter, Salvor?" the voice asked.

"Oh." I sat in silence for a few seconds. "I don't know what's going to happen to me now." I dropped my hands into my lap and continued in a quiet voice, "I've done some pretty terrible things up to this point, and once we return to Mars, the best I can hope for is to be arrested and sent away to some prison floating around a far-flung ice ball."

More typing.

"We can't have the man that returned our Promise rot in a cell, now, can we?" the voice said. "Perhaps I can help you out on that front. How would you like a job?"

In my head Merv, piped up. "Dopamine has increased and serotonin levels are at three-hundred-twenty nanograms per millilitre. Also, our bladder is at fifty-nine-percent capacity."

That conversation aboard the Avius happened almost four months ago. Since then, I've come to enjoy the company of Elios Ukam. The man is not only my saviour, he's also rich and well-connected. I guess that's what happens when you own one of the most successful shipyards on Mars.

The Promise Kept

Once we got back to the red planet, Elios gave me refuge at his personal complex. While I recovered, he bought me a new identity and new call codes for Merv. Salvor Gupta was officially dead. He burned up in the atmosphere of Titan. I am now Arjun Singh, personal pilot to Mr. Ukam. I get to fly one of the swankiest crafts out there, my faithful dog figurine sitting on the top of the cockpit console, agreeing with everything I say, unlike Merv. When I'm not doing that, I hang around the shipyard, looking at the ships being built. Elios even gave me a place of my own in his complex. It's really nice - I can gaze up through the dome at night and see the moons and ships flying past.

As for Project Promise, the prototype had been in good shape when the box was opened, complete with plans intact. Two months after the prototype was received by Elios' team at the shipyards, the first ten were ready to be trialled. So far, the results look promising; the fetuses are all developing normally, and Elios has plans to make thousands more. He's dedicated a whole area of the shipyards to it. He's being hailed as a hero; I don't mind if he gets all the credit, to be honest.

Now that he has new codes, Merv and I can slip in and out of any orbiter without raising alarms, but he's still the same pain in the ass he's always been. He continues to remind me to exercise and take a piss, but something in his programming has started making him bring up my old identity every now-and-then, comparing my new life to the old one, and I have a hard time enough remembering my new name without him tossing the old one around in my brain.

Maybe this is his way of coping with the changes we went through, coming to terms with having to kill in order to continue our operation - accessing memories from before the day we docked at Ring 4 on Homestead. I know that sometimes, when I stand in my little piece of Mars, changing from my crisp white pilot's uniform to something that doesn't make me stand out like a sore thumb in the common areas, I linger at my multi-angle mirrors, gaze fixed upon the scar that travels across my lower left back. Sure, I could have the scar removed with plastic surgery, but it reminds me of who I once was, what I have been through.

Oh, and the rumours that were going around about Janice returning to Mars? They're true. One day, I'm walking through one of the long above ground passageways that connects the living areas of Elonton City together, minding my own business. The passageway's transparent elongated dome gives great views of the Sol-rise as the star crests the ridges of the slight crater the city was built in, and I stop to take in the sight of it.

Sol-rise here on Mars is much different than back on Earth. The light is weaker and colours different, illuminating the sky in bright blues and whites, not the familiar red and oranges from back home.

"It's beautiful, isn't it?" I muse to myself.

"The colour is due to the fact that very fine dust in the Martian atmosphere is the right size so that blue light penetrates the atmosphere slightly more efficiently than all the other colours," Merv drones. I roll my eyes and smile.

"You're a real killjoy, you know that?" I mutter.

I become aware that I'm no longer alone in the corridor; two distinct voices can be heard coming from the direction I'm headed in. One voice stands out, the same voice I heard begging me for forgiveness as I had lain on a cold, metallic office floor, unable to move or talk to my AI.

I freeze. As Janice comes closer, I see a companion reflected in the corridor windows, walking next to Janice's mechanised walking frame; they're engrossed in a conversation about the price of scavenged solar panels. I can tell that the other person is a new salvager; they are too young, too well kept, and Janice is fleecing them, undercutting them sixty-percent of what a good deal should be.

"If you agree to those terms, just come with me to my office," Janice says, the sound of her voice making the little hairs on my neck stand up. I will never forget that voice for as long as I live. "We'll plug into my desk and complete the transaction via AI."

They are no more than a few metres from me now, as I stand looking out the tunnel dome at the Sol-rise. I long to hurt her and I feel the anger in me rising with every word she says, with every hollow foot-fall her walking frame makes.

I ball my hands into fists.

"Our heart-rate has increased and the force of our clenched jaws is well over thirteen-hundred newtons," Merv said. "May we be reminded of how gracious our patron Mr. Ukam has been? We do not believe he would be as willing to help if we attacked a fellow Martian with no provocation."

I let out a long, deep breath. When Merv is right, he's right.

"You know," I say nonchalantly as I spin to face the two people now directly behind my back, "I wouldn't settle for less than ten times what she's offering you." I smirk at the new salvager and can instantly see their face reflect the thoughts going through their mind. Blue outlines of the two appear in my vision, and I learn the newbie's name -Unum Novum. Human. I'm right; they've only been salvaging for a few months.

Janice flashes a look of anger at me, her small parasitic face starting to mouth silent words, its eyes searching blindly along the tunnel for the source of its host's fury. Anger quickly turns to recognition, then fear, as Janice recognises the face behind the voice.

"Salvor?" she hisses.

"I think you might need to have a diagnostic run against your AI," I say coyly. "My name is Arjun Singh." I give Unum a look, raising my eyebrows and insinuating that Janice might be crazy. They nod back slightly in agreement, their AI showing them my new name, not Salvor.

"No, no, I'm sure. You're Salvor," Janice whispers, the look of fear frozen in her eyes. Her second face is babbling away in a voice that would never be heard, most likely repeating my new name displayed on her own vision overlay. Janice looks like she has seen a ghost. "You're dead."

I say nothing.

"I appreciate your offer," Unum finally says after a few seconds of awkward silence, "but I think I'll explore my options elsewhere." They turn and walk away quickly in the direction from which they and Janice had come. Janice is still standing there in her walking frame, mouth agape and staring.

"Well, looks like you've lost a customer," I say. "That's too bad. I hope it doesn't become a habit."

I turn and start walking away from her, in the same direction Unum went. I stop a few metres down the tunnel and turn back.

"I'll be seeing you around," I say in a friendly voice. "Janice? Was it?"

I give a big grin and continue down the tunnel, never looking back to see what her reaction would be. I'm happy that the ghost of Salvor could be useful after all.

"Although our serotonin levels have increased by sixteen-percent, we do not believe that was the wisest course of action," Merv says.

"Don't worry too much about it," I murmur. "Bring up my credit balance and let's find out where Unum went. I have a feeling I'm about to make a new friend."

I'm not going to worry, Merv will have my back, and that's something I can always count on.

Don't miss out!

Visit the website below and you can sign up to receive emails whenever Matthew Villeneuve publishes a new book. There's no charge and no obligation.

https://books2read.com/r/B-A-ZBNT-DAUZB

BOOKS 2 READ

Connecting independent readers to independent writers.

www.ingramcontent.com/pod-product-compliance
Lightning Source LLC
Chambersburg PA
CBHW061701130726
47996CB00006B/2112